JUSTICE DENIED

MARK O'CONNELL

TATE PUBLISHING
AND ENTERPRISES, LLC

3 0 8 0 4 5 7 5 4

Published by Tate Publishing & Enterprises, LLC
127 E. Trade Center Terrace | Mustang, Oklahoma 73064 USA
1.888.361.9473 | www.tatepublishing.com

Tate Publishing is committed to excellence in the publishing industry. The company reflects the philosophy established by the founders, based on Psalm 68:11,

"The Lord gave the word and great was the company of those who published it."

Book design copyright © 2016 by Tate Publishing, LLC. All rights reserved.
Cover design by Joana Quilantang
Interior design by Manolito Bastasa

Published in the United States of America

ISBN: 978-1-68352-341-3
1. Fiction / Crime
2. Fiction / Family Life
16.06.09

Based on the true story of a family's
tragic and mysterious death

To G.
May you have the blessed assurance that God will judge them all

CONTENTS

AUTHOR'S NOTE

I WROTE THIS book based on the copious information I received from the person for whom this book is dedicated. She enjoyed a close relationship with the victim, an older sister, and soon, following her death, spent a lot of time and energy conducting her own brand of investigation. Her recollection of the events is vivid and precise; her instincts and intuition are reliable; and her loyalty to family is unquestionable. It was, however, necessary to change the names of the people involved to protect their identity, including her own, recognizing the potential repercussions to her or her family in the event future evidence is developed and cases are reopened for further investigation.

Because this book is a novel based on a true story, the author—with the consent from the reporting family member—took some liberty in developing characters in an attempt to breathe life into the story and keep the reader intrigued. I tried to keep in mind, when developing dialogue between characters, what was characteristic of the culture and some of the popular lingo of the time periods that the story spans.

What is not subjective, and what cannot be disputed, is the fact that both her sister and her sister's son died; that no one was ever prosecuted for their deaths; and that it is doubtful that anyone ever will be. Still, for this family of rural origin, who has always enjoyed close bonds, it is a story that needs telling.

As a Christian who trusts in God, I believe that God inspired me to write this story. If you enjoy the book, to God goes the glory.

To the family, I offer this passage from the Holy Scripture: "Grace and peace be yours in abundance through the knowledge of God and of Jesus our Lord" (2 Pet. 1:2, NIV).

PROLOGUE

TERESA DODSON GREW up in rural Madison County, Virginia, where her parents—James (known to his family and friends as Jimmy) and Martha Dodson—raised a large family. Teresa was the third of their eight children and witnessed her share of her father's drinking and his emotional abuse toward her mother. She remembers all too well how her father was often absent from the home, which left her mother as the sole nurturer of the children. Teresa was always thankful for the love of her mother. Everyone considered her a saint. But not even a saintly mother could forever endure the ongoing abuse by an alcoholic and often-absent husband. The couple eventually divorced.

Martha Dodson worked two jobs to feed and clothe the children and to make sure that Christmas and other holidays were happy times for the family.

By 2005, Teresa had already married and divorced with three children of her own.

That year, Christmas was anything but joyful.

She spent the day alone with one thing on her mind: the safety of her children. They were with their father, who had agreed to bring them back on December 26. In November, he had been released from jail and asked her if he could take the children to his home to visit his family. He swore he was a changed man; she had heard that before. He had been incarcerated a few times, and after each release he vowed he had changed. But this time, he was more persuasive, so she relented and allowed him to take them. He took them on the twenty-third, and by agreement, he would have them for three days.

She fretted for their safety. Would he harm them? Would his family? Would she ever see them again? These questions could not be answered then, so she spent a pensive Christmas consumed with worries over their welfare. The next day, she called her sister, Jenny, and told her that he had not brought the children home. Teresa and Jenny talked extensively. Teresa could always rely on Jenny to be a good listener and a loyal sister. Though Jenny assured her that the kids would be okay, deep down Jenny knew differently. She also worried about Teresa; she had never heard her talk quite this way.

Two days after Christmas, it was back to work for Teresa, but on this day, the police telephoned Jenny from Teresa's place of employment because Teresa had not shown up for work. After a number of years of perfect attendance, she was inexplicably absent. The officer asked Jenny, "When was the last time you spoke to your sister?"

Jenny replied, "Last night."

He said, "She didn't come to work. We have reason to believe she may be in danger."

So did Jenny. "I'm going to her house," she told the officer.

It took Jenny only eight minutes to travel from her work site to Teresa's home. Those eight minutes tormented her. She did not believe this story would end well.

The coldness she felt within nearly matched the frigid outdoor temperature of 24 degrees. She pulled into Teresa's driveway, slammed the gear into park, and jumped out of her car. As she walked the few steps to the door, she heard the sound of thinly breaking ice with each step she took. The ground was frozen; the wind was blustery, and it seemed to burn her face. The volume of the television had been turned way up, annoyingly so. She banged and banged on the door, but no answer. She looked through a window and saw her sister's purse on the table. Finding a door ajar, she went in. She called for Teresa, but no answer.

Jenny walked down the hallway and soon made the discovery she had feared most. Teresa was lying facedown in the hallway just outside her bedroom door; her body was cold. Both fists were clinched. In one hand was her hairbrush and in the other the telephone. Jenny heard the busy signal. Teresa had tried to call for help.

It was too late. Younger sister Jenny took a deep breath, exhaled, and called 911. As she waited for dispatch to answer, she thought, *Oh my God, what about those kids?* They were so many miles away, and Jenny felt helpless. But this family was close-knit, and seeing Teresa lying dead in the hallway of her own home stirred the combative juices that already flowed in Jenny's veins.

Intuitively, Jenny always knew that something bad would happen to Teresa, yet she was always helpless to do anything to save her.

Teresa's death was tragic. Hers was the first, but not the last this family would see. Years have since passed, and the person/s responsible has not yet been brought to justice, leaving family members and friends to ponder, how long must evil flourish?

1

A SAVING GRACE

A LIGHT RAIN fell softly on the tin roof of the family home as Teresa and her siblings tried to sleep.

The gentleness of the rain helped only a little, since she and her siblings could hear their father yelling at their mother in their bedroom. This happened often, and Teresa wondered if his abuse would escalate from verbal to physical.

So did her younger sister.

"Why is Daddy so angry?" asked Katie.

"I don't know," said Teresa. "Try to go to sleep."

"Do you think he will get mad at us?"

"I don't think so. Momma will know what to do."

Katie soon cried herself to sleep; Teresa had a disturbing dream.

Their mother always stood in the gap for them. She took the abuse from her husband and would have laid down her life for any of her children had he ever directed his abuse toward them.

Without their mother, Teresa and her siblings would have lived a life of constant turmoil and uncertainty. Aside from the obvious abuse, their father was also unfaithful. Though their mother never talked about it or let on that she knew, Teresa and her siblings were keenly aware of his antics. His sexual appetite was often satisfied by a woman who lived just a few miles away.

Known to his family and friends as Jimmy, James Dodson grew up in the country and had struggled to find his own identity. His father drank heavily, gambled away his limited earnings, and even took food out of the mouths of Jimmy and his brothers and sisters to show them who was boss. Their mother stood by helplessly as Ralph Dodson meted out his cruelty. He indiscriminately landed backhanded slaps to the faces of his wife and their children. No one knew who would be the next victim.

Outside the home, Jimmy found little refuge in school. He hated it; his grades were bad, and he had no interest in sports or music. The only reason he went to school was to get away from his father. After school, he found some reward in taking automotive repair classes. This would become his vocation and escape.

When Jimmy started a family with Martha, his idea of being a father and a husband was tainted by what his father had modeled.

He drank hard, abused his wife, and had affairs with other women. At least when he was absent, the abuse stopped.

When Teresa's grandfather came around, he liked to drink and to play bluegrass music. Because of her dislike of him, Teresa developed a disdain for bluegrass music. She could tolerate any other genre of music; but bluegrass, thanks to her grandfather, had a vulgar ring to it.

With little support from their father, Teresa and her siblings turned to their mother, who worked two jobs, tended a ten-acre garden, canned fruits and vegetables, and served as a seamstress for a well-to-do family.

The children did their share of chores. They picked the fruits, shelled peas and beans, and helped store the canned items on shelves in the basement.

Teresa never forgot the example of a godly mother, and as an adult, she recalled a conversation with her mother that she would never forget.

"Momma, why do you work so hard?" she asked.

"There's always a lot to be done," was her mother's response.

"Do you ever worry about what's going to happen to all of us?"

"A parent always worries, but the good Lord has been good to us."

"How can you say that, knowing what daddy has been like?"

"The Lord has a plan for us all. One day, he will have to explain to God why he acted this way."

"I hate what he's done to you."

"One day you'll get married and have children of your own."

That evoked mixed feelings in Teresa. The idea of being a mother sounded good, but being a wife might mean being married to a tyrant.

Oh my God, she thought. *What if I end up with someone like my daddy?*

Through the childhood and adolescent years, Teresa and her siblings did what most children in rural America do: they went to school and did chores at home.

They attended the public schools in their county. Teresa always did well in school. Her favorite subjects were English and science; and she graduated from the local high school where she was an honor roll student.

During all four years of high school, she dated the same guy. He was a year older than her, and he proposed to her out of high school. Teresa wasn't so sure about marriage; instead, she moved in with him to see how things would go.

Just a few months into the live-in arrangement, their relationship came to an abrupt halt when Teresa came upon some pictures that showed him intimately involved with another man.

It would have been painful enough for him to have left her for another woman; Teresa would have been naturally jealous. But for him to be involved with another man? She struggled to reconcile his actions with her traditional upbringing.

This shocking discovery caused Teresa a serious emotional setback. Devastated, she opted to move back home with her mother and siblings.

But her father had not changed; he was still mean, still abusing alcohol, and still chasing women. His actions brought to mind the expression Teresa had heard people use: "Leopards never change their spots." Teresa simply could not get along with him. It was time to move again. This time, she moved to her maternal grandmother's house, which later became hers.

Following in the footsteps of her mother, Teresa developed a solid work ethic and began working for a local factory right out of high school. The familiarity of factory work suited her well. She knew her job, did it well, and never missed out on the stress that comes with more responsibility. She even took pride in having a perfect attendance record. There were times when illness, which would have kept others at home, did not deter Teresa from getting to work.

But a good work ethic wasn't enough. Teresa felt a tremendous void in her life. She desired a life partner.

2

LOOKING FOR LOVE

To her coworkers and friends, Teresa's academic success and solid work ethic were good indicators of a well-adjusted individual. A closer inspection indicated differently. Teresa suffered from low self-esteem. The absence of a good father figure had an adverse affect on her self-confidence and outlook in life. His treatment of her mother hurt her as a child and made her angry as an adult. It also stereotyped what she thought men were like. She learned early on the value of speaking one's mind and expressing the truth no matter how harsh it sounded. Better to get things out in the open than to hide them she thought. It was better to tell something the way it is rather than to tell someone what they wanted to hear.

Teresa had a good command of the English language. She dealt with everyone fairly and exercised the sort of diplomacy that made her win most everyone over. Rarely did she use profanity, but when she did, people took notice.

But like her father and her grandfather before her, Teresa turned to alcohol—and sometimes illegal drugs—to alleviate the pain she felt. She started going to bars when she was twenty-one. There, she met men whose interest in her was driven largely by their sexual appetites, but she wasn't the type of woman to jump into bed with just any man. The few times she did, she naively thought she would feel loved. But the morning after those nightly interludes fueled by alcohol, and sometimes illegal drugs, left her feeling hollow.

Most of her trips to the local bars were on the weekends, especially Fridays, because those nights signaled the end of a long workweek and the hope of finding that special someone whom she would eventually marry and start a family with.

Teresa missed out on the conventional wisdom that the best places to find a partner were either in school or in church. She wasn't attending college, and she rarely made time for church. Even at work, no one piqued her interest. Internet dating had not yet become in vogue, so the bars were the likely choice for socialization and meeting someone of the opposite sex.

She learned the hard lessons that come from quick physical interactions with strangers whose backgrounds and true intentions were uncertain at best, and often purely unknown.

At one of her favorite hangouts, the Rapid River, Teresa knew the bartenders, the customers, the songs on the jukebox; and she even became an adept billiards player. Shooting pool with some expertise caused any customer's stock to rise in the eyes of their fellow imbibers.

When Teresa came into the Rapid River, the bartender greeted her with his customary "Good evening." Of the bartenders who worked there, Teresa liked all of them except one. His name was Mark, and she never forgot his sarcastic quip the night before Halloween one year. As Teresa was talking to one of her fellow customers about what they were going to dress up as, she remembered telling the other patron, "I'm going to be a witch." Mark was listening to their conversation and as he walked away, Teresa heard him say, "Going to be?" She never forgot that. When Mark was working, she did not greet him with anything but "Lite draft."

Even Mark quickly poured her favorite draft beer, and Teresa would always pay as she ordered. At that time, a draft beer cost only 90 cents.

Once the beer was in front of her, Teresa would quickly scan the crowd to survey the prospects for the evening.

Perhaps some new gentleman—clean and wearing a sharp attire—might grace her presence. That almost seemed idealistic; in reality, it was usually the same crowd—the blue-collar workers still clad in their soiled clothing from a hard day's work who came in, eager to quench a powerful thirst and with loving on their minds, the kind that you steal for a night and wave good-bye to in the morning.

Deep down, Teresa longed for more: something that would satisfy, something that would make her feel good.

In the dimly lit bar, smoke filled the air, and the familiar sound of the most popular songs rang in the ears. It didn't take long for a song to go from popular to well overplayed, but even then, it sounded good to the regular customers who had found a safe haven and a place to call a second home.

Teresa met a lot of former school mates at this bar, many of whom tended to rest on their high school laurels as though life had begun and reached its pinnacle with those. Most had little ambition to pursue the finer things in life, and many lacked the true self-confidence to venture even a little outside their comfort zones.

Aside from the usual former jocks, roughnecks, and blowhards, occasionally some new patron would come in, and Teresa was quick to take notice.

To her friends and family, Teresa was known for being bold and not afraid to speak her mind. She did not hesitate to tell something the way she thought it was, even if it sounded a little harsh. And the guys in bars could take it. They all seemed to have that rough exterior. Being hyper-sensitive would never be a strong suit in a bar.

Still, the best way for a guy to talk to Teresa was for him to initiate contact. Maybe she was old school in this way. She looked for the man to be a little thoughtful and avoid the usual pickup lines. But if she was feeling especially lonely, even the corny pickup lines would have some useful effect.

When a man looked her way, she felt the nervousness that comes in anticipation of talking to a perfect stranger. Invariably, she lit her next cigarette. Sometimes, a thoughtful fellow might anticipate as much and be quick with the draw of his lighter or matchbook. If he were really thoughtful, he would let the sulfur burn off the lit match before he directed the flame toward her cigarette. If she missed that cue, he might say, "I got the sulfur." Those were the little things she relished. Thoughtfulness: a concept often lost in this type of setting where occasional fights broke out and Teresa and other innocent bystanders would look for concealment from the flying glasses or ashtrays that were hurled as missiles.

Ordinarily, this bar enjoyed peace, and as long as the fisticuffs were out of her sight, Teresa was happy.

She had other things to think about, including the self-doubt about her physical attractiveness. She was tall and thin, the job at the factory having burned its share of calories; but she did not exercise or play sports. Her hair was dark, and her upper lip was thin. To those who looked into her eyes, they could see the pain behind the smile. A dimly lit bar was actually her ally.

In the morning, both she and her lover would see the real picture.

But no one looked to the morning after; it was always the night that offered life and the hope of some sense of fulfillment.

In this crowd, people appeared to be happy, and Teresa felt right at home.

In this bar, people drank, told jokes, interacted with others, played pool, and popped quarters in the jukebox, which was the only source of music.

One night, as one of her favorite songs—"Lonely Too Long" by Patty Loveless—was playing, she caught sight of a stranger never seen before who came in with another man, a friend. The two of them bellied up to the bar and ordered two bottles of beer.

Teresa had a good feeling about this. She turned to a friend and told her that tonight they may want to operate in tandem. Who knew where the night might lead. Someone might get lucky.

One of the men approached her. He wore a white shirt with a wide collar and a necklace with a cross. The cross, or any other religious symbol, always seemed out of place in such a setting.

"Can I buy you a drink?" he asked.

Reluctant to smile, Teresa said, "Sure."

"What are you drinking?

"Lite draft."

"Bartender, bring this lady a Lite draft and whatever her friend is drinking. It's on me."

Teresa's friend liked red eyes, which in honky-tonks meant beer mixed with tomato juice.

Her friend Debbie was cute in the face, but short and sporting a few extra pounds.

The man buying the drinks was Mike. His friend Dale watched and was prepared to follow Mike's cues.

Teresa thought the same thing she always thought when she met a man for the first time: *Maybe he's the one.*

Though Mike had the all-too-common beer gut, he had an otherwise-strong physique, giving the impression he had been an athlete in his day. His hair was jet-black and curly, and he had a noticeable, but not unattractive, gap between his two front teeth.

"Can I join you?" Mike asked Teresa. She mustered a quick smile and said yes. Dale then inched his way toward Debbie, hoping for the same reception. He didn't have to wait long. Debbie helped move the stool away from the bar to make his welcome a little easier.

Debbie and Dale immediately hit it off, and soon Debbie was giggling.

Teresa noticed but focused on Mike. After all, the two of them had just been matched.

"Don't think I've seen you here before." Teresa mentioned to Mike.

"No," he said. "They say there's a first time for everything."

"Sounds like the name of a song," quipped Teresa.

"What kind of music do you like?" asked Mike.

"Anything but bluegrass."

"Any requests for the jukebox?" he asked.

"How about 'Islands in the Stream,'*" she replied. Teresa and a number of other customers, almost exclusively female, enjoyed singing along when it played.

As Mike made his way to the jukebox, Teresa looked over at Debbie to gauge her situation. She and Dale were enjoying each other. Teresa figured there was no need to interrupt a good thing. She waited for Mike to return.

When he did, he asked her if she liked to shoot pool.

"Yes," she said.

"How about we challenge the table for a game of doubles?" he asked.

---

* "Islands in the Stream" was a popular country song performed by Dolly Parton and Kenny Rogers.

"Sure."

Mike wrote his name on the chalkboard, which indi-cated the order of players.

A couple of games later, it was Mike's turn. He asked the reigning champion if he would consent to a game of doubles. He agreed and turned to a friend and regular patron for the honor.

Mike told Teresa, "We're up."

In this bar, the protocol called for the game of eight-ball, and players had to call their pockets. Also, the chal-lenger racked the balls, and the champion broke them.

When the champion broke this rack, three balls found their way to three different pockets. Two of the three were striped balls, which became the champion's selection.

On his next shot, he sank the twelve-ball, but the cue ball rolled out of range for the next shot, and he played it defensively.

Mike looked to Teresa to see who of the two of them would go first. Teresa gave the nod to Mike. He imme-diately went to work and sank two balls following two strokes. He then missed on his third, which gave the turn to the champion's partner.

He made a couple of good shots and reduced the num-ber of striped balls on the table to two, which left Mike and Teresa four solid balls remaining.

Teresa took her turn. She had an easy shot on the six-ball and sank it in one of the side pockets.

The four- and seven-balls happened to be in close proximity to a corner pocket, and she called both in the corner.

Following her stroke, both went in the pocket and the crowd, who had recently tuned in, erupted with approval.

But on her next shot, she was out of range and played it defensively, meaning she stayed away from the eight-ball and did not allow the cue ball to find its way to an unwelcome pocket. In other words, she avoided a scratch.

The champion had two more striped balls to sink before he could eye in on the eight-ball. He dropped the 13 ball in the side pocket and then missed his next shot.

The table was down to four balls—the cue, the eight-ball, one solid, and one stripe. The match was even at this point.

Mike lined up his and Teresa's last ball and sank it on a long shot but left the cue well out of range of the eight-ball. Mike played it safe, and, after a defensive shot, turned the game over to their opponents.

The champion's partner sank their last ball and then took the game's first direct shot on the eight-ball but missed by a bunch.

It was Teresa's turn. She had a long-range shot at the 8 and a 50/50 chance of nailing the shot or scratching the cue.

Her heart rate accelerated as the crowd now focused on her. She could feel her palms sweating, so she used some chalk to make them dry. She quickly conferred with Mike, who said, "You can do this."

Like a golfer lining up a putt, Teresa lined up the cue ball and the eight-ball and then wheeled into position. To her, it felt as though her heart was beating at an all-time high. She knew everyone was watching. If it had been anything else, her nerves would have let her down. But this was pool, and she had some well-deserved confidence. She called the pocket and then stroked the cue. It made its way to the eight-ball, which it struck. The eight-ball headed toward its target, but Teresa had too much behind this stroke. The eight-ball caromed around the pocket like a basketball in the cylinder and hit the wall and made its way to the center of the table. Meanwhile, the cue ball narrowly missed going into a pocket of its own.

Teresa felt the disappointment that comes in a would-be clutch moment. Her face turned red with embarrassment. Mike said, "It's okay, don't worry about it."

But she knew he was disappointed. Nobody likes to lose, especially a game of pool in a honky-tonk.

The champion and his partner were in excellent position to sink the 8 and remain champions.

The champion quickly did so, and Mike and Teresa congratulated them and walked back to the bar.

Clearly dejected, Teresa felt like a failure. A sense of sadness came over her. This emotion had been no stranger in her life.

Mike was disappointed but quickly asked her, "Would you like to get high?"

"Definitely," said Teresa. "Like what?

"Some powder," he said, referring to cocaine.

"Why don't you ask your friend if she wants to join us," he added. "We can go in Dale's car."

Teresa leaned over to Debbie and mentioned as much. Debbie was only too happy to go. A good jolt would do them all good.

Teresa motioned for the bartender to hold their drinks; they would be back.

The bartender smiled. He knew what that meant. The customer takes a break from drinking and smokes a joint or sniffs a couple of lines of cocaine to enhance the buzz, then returns for more drinks a little happier following the illicit indulgence.

The two couples left the bar and headed to Dale's car. He pointed the way to his 1976 Chevrolet Nova, baby blue and with four doors for four people.

Dale hopped in the driver's seat and Debbie in the front passenger seat. Mike sat behind Dale and Teresa behind Debbie.

"Are we safe here?" Dale asked.

"We might want to travel down a back road," said Teresa. "The cops come through here some. They know what people do here."

Dale laughed and put the car in reverse. "Tell me where to go," he said.

Teresa directed him down a back road that was secluded and not well lit. She knew of a sort of unofficial wayside where they could pull off and take a hit or two.

Once there, Dale maneuvered to a stop that would allow him to pull out quickly if the need arose. Once the headlights were out, it was pitch dark.

Dale turned the interior light on long enough for Dale to use a razor blade to break up the cocaine and spread the lines that the four of them would snort.

Mike reached into his front jeans pocket; pulled out a baggie of cocaine, a little over a gram; and immediately went to work. After cutting out the lines, he offered the first to Teresa. She was smart enough to say, "You go first." Mike did, and then turned the makeshift plate over to Teresa, who used the same rolled-up $1 bill he had just used. When she snorted the line, the gratification was instant. She knew *this* was good stuff.

Next, Debbie took her turn, and then Dale. Soon everyone began talking—excessively. Using cocaine had that effect on most people; and once someone started talking, it was difficult for someone else to get a word in edgewise.

But it was all good until Mike dropped a bombshell. During the conversation, he accidentally mentioned his wife.

A wife? Teresa thought. *How could you?*

He tried to gracefully recover and exit the conversation, but it was too late. The word was out, and despite the euphoria that comes from using cocaine, Teresa felt a drop in emotion and needed another jolt.

Dale picked up on the drop and told Mike to lay out another line.

Mike kept talking. The more he talked, the less credibility he had with Teresa. The damage was done. Mike was not the one she was looking for.

Dale had to tell Mike again to lay out another line. Mike apologized for the delay and then went to work. This time around, Teresa chomped at the bit to go first. This second jolt was just what she needed.

When the plate was clear, Teresa suggested they go back to the bar for another drink.

Dale offered to take them back to his place where he had liquor and a pool table.

Debbie was excited at the prospect, but Teresa knew this was a dead-end evening for her as far as Mike was concerned. Yes, she was lonely. And yes, she wanted a man. But even her sense of desperation at times would not cause her to cross the line; she would not have sexual relations with a married man, no matter what he said.

And Mike was a smooth talker. He had played this game many times in the past with its share of success. He had no reason to think tonight would be any different, but he underestimated Teresa.

Teresa didn't want to go to Dale's home. She knew Mike would make advances, but she also recognized that Debbie and Dale were hitting it off, and she didn't want to be Debbie's downer.

It was time to have a girl talk, the kind that usually takes place in a restroom. Teresa suggested they go back to the bar. She needed to use the bathroom.

The scheme worked. Dale and Mike agreed, and Dale drove back to the Rapid River. The girls went in ahead of the men, and Teresa grabbed Debbie by the arm and said, "We need to talk." She ushered Debbie to the bathroom and immediately expressed her concerns.

"Mike is married. What a jerk. He acted like he was single."

"What did you expect?" asked Debbie. "Aren't most guys in here jerks?"

"I thought he was different," said Teresa.

"They are all different at first."

"What about Dale?"

"He's great," said Debbie. "But I'm not going to his house without you. He's fun, but I hardly know the guy."

"I don't want to rain on your parade, but Mike is married. I don't wanna get involved with a married man."

"What do we tell them?"

"We tell them thanks for the drinks and the high but we have to get up early in the morning."

"Okay."

When the ladies approached the bar, they were surprised to find that Dale and Mike had disappeared.

While Dale exited with a clear conscience, Mike realized the folly in his loose tongue and was too embarrassed to be seen again. Another good jolt would ease that feeling. He would cut a couple more lines for him and Dale and then head off to another bar.

The girls went to the bar to say good night to Joel, the bartender at the time.

"I see y'all are back," he said. "I think your new friends decided to vamoose."

"Yeah," said Teresa. "Guess it's true: easy come easy go."

The clichés continued.

"Maybe your new friends had bigger fish to fry," said Joel.

Teresa added a new twist to the old expression when she said, "Glad we weren't the fish."

"You wanna beer? It's on me," said Joel.

"No, thanks," said Teresa. "Think I've had enough tonight." Under her breath, she uttered, "Enough of everything."

The girls went home. Debbie hoped she might see Dale again while Teresa reasoned that meeting Mike was indicative of the future she faced: she would never meet Mr. Right.

After a relatively uneventful rest of the weekend, she returned to work on Monday. Her coworkers noted that she looked particularly glum.

One of them asked her, "Who shit in your cornflakes?"

"Very funny," said Teresa. "What the hell is wrong with men?"

"Oh, that again," said her coworker. "A lot of them are jerks, but don't give up. You'll find someone."

Teresa hated those words. "You'll find someone." It made it sound like she was desperate, dependent, and would latch on to someone for relief. Teresa thought she was above that. She vowed not to go back to the Rapid River for a while. The same old stiffs went there. She would try an alternate bar, a sort of change of venue.

The workweek had just begun. Four more days until Friday, and she would hear the song designated for that day: "It's Finally Friday" by county music legend George Jones.

When Friday came, Teresa punched out on the time clock, got in her always-reliable Toyota Corolla, and turned on the radio. Within a few minutes, that song played. She felt immediately better. She knew every word and sang along. The weekend was here. Friday nights were always special, and tonight she would head south to a bar she had never been. Rumor had it that the Oasis was a hot spot of activity. She would go there.

That decision would change her life forever.

3

THE FATEFUL ENCOUNTER

FIRST THINGS FIRST: Teresa drove home to shower, change clothes, and grab a bite to eat before going out. Since she was making her first trip to a different bar, she called Debbie to see if she was interested in going. Debbie already had plans. Sometime before Dale and Mike had bolted from the Rapid River, Dale had asked for Debbie's telephone number. During the week Dale called Debbie and the two of them made plans for Friday night.

Debbie didn't alert Teresa. She figured her contact with Dale would only serve to remind Teresa of Mike.

So Teresa would make this trip alone.

The longer drive to Charlottesville would at least be a diversion, and maybe more. Not knowing what to expect added a little excitement to the drive. Maybe tonight would be the night.

She knew she was at least guaranteed good service by the bartenders. Women always received good service when the bartenders were guys, and most of the bartenders she knew were guys.

By the time she left home it was 7:00 p.m. The approximate one-hour drive to the bar would put her at her location by 8:00 p.m.

She got in her car, backed out of the driveway, and turned the radio on, hoping to hear some favorite songs to accompany her along the way.

As each mile passed, she changed stations, hoping to find a song she liked. Finding none, she reminded herself that a cold draft beer would have its usual satisfying effects, especially after another long and hard workweek. Factory work is tedious, and she and her coworkers spent a lot of time on their feet.

The barstool would prove its usual welcome. The music would soothe the senses, and the beer would go down easy. These were the little things to look forward to even if she was going about life alone.

When she reached her destination, there was plenty of parking available. Most bars didn't get busy until the later hours in the evening.

She pulled out her compact to look in its mirror for a last look at her face before going on. Satisfied with how she looked, she exited her vehicle and went inside.

Once in, she immediately noticed a huge dance floor. She didn't dance at the Rapid River. There was no designated place for that. When people danced there, it was a sign they had consumed too much of something.

She found a good seat at the bar. Almost immediately, the bartender came over and asked what she would like.

"Lite draft please."

Moments later, she had her first beer in front of her. That first sip was always the best. She soon scanned the crowd to check out the prospects. Not much yet, but the night was young.

Midway through her second beer, a gentleman approached her and asked her to dance.

She agreed and the two of them danced to "Celebrate,"** which was an easy song to dance to, and it felt good to be moving to music.

After the song, her dance partner thanked her, and she returned to the bar. There was a mirror on the wall in front of where she sat, and when she looked into it, she saw a

---

** "Celebrate" was recorded by Kool and the Gang.

man sitting behind her who was looking at her. He had a broad smile, and he didn't take his eyes off of her.

She soon turned away, wanting to play her cards right. She hoped he was impressed enough with her that he would soon initiate a conversation. He did not disappoint.

She watched as he walked toward her. He was of medium height and a small frame, but muscular and attractive. He quickly introduced himself. She felt nervous, but in a good way.

"Hi, I'm Rick," he said, with a heavy odor of alcohol on his breath.

"I'm Teresa."

"Don't think I've seen you here before."

"No, first time. What about you?"

"Oh, this is my favorite watering hole," he said with a laugh.

"I guess everyone has their favorite," replied Teresa.

"Where you coming from tonight?"

"Madison."

"Madison? I know about Madison. I live in Orange."

"It's country."

"Country is good. And it certainly looks good tonight," he said, trying to be a little clever.

Teresa smiled, and actually giggled a little. She welcomed the flattery.

"You know, this beer isn't doing it for me," said Rick. "Do you do anything other than beer?"

"You mean like pot or coke?"

"Yeah like that."

"Sure, what do you have in mind?"

"You want to burn one?"

"Yeah, that would be nice."

Rick was a regular here and motioned the bartender to come over. When he did, Rick said, "Dave, hold our drinks. We'll be back."

"You got it," Dave replied.

Rick and Teresa went outside, where he escorted her to his car and opened the passenger door and let her in just like a gentleman would do. Rick felt safe smoking a joint here in the parking lot. He reached inside his jacket pocket and pulled out a pack of rolling papers and then a single wrap. Next, he reached inside the console and pulled out a container, which was formerly a 35mm film holder. Those were popular then. They were small enough to easily conceal but large enough to carry a sufficient quantity of marijuana for an evening. And if the owner had to ditch the stash, the loss wouldn't be so great.

It was obvious to Teresa that Rick had rolled more than his share of joints. He licked the adhesive to secure it and then licked the outside of the adhesive from end to end to ensure its contact. Next, he took his cigarette lighter and carefully heated the area he had wetted to make sure it was dry.

It was now ready to smoke. He lit one end, took in a deep toke, and held in the smoke while he passed the joint to her.

When she took a toke, it felt good—really good.

She knew this was quality weed, and she liked its effects.

After passing the joint back and forth a few times, both agreed they had had enough at the time; and Rick extinguished its fire by sticking the tip into a well-salivated mouth. What was left, the roach, he put in the ashtray.

Time to go back inside.

They returned to the bar, where Dave brought them a couple of beers "on the house." The two of them were feeling the effects of the marijuana, and rather than making them both mellow, it actually enhanced their conversation. They immediately recognized they had much in common.

But Teresa recognized that Rick's accent was not as thick as that of her kinfolk and her coworkers. "Where are you from?"

"I was born in New York."

But before he could continue, Teresa interrupted: "You're a Yankee?"

"No," said Rick. "I was born there, but when I was three, we moved to Florida. I lived there for the most part."

"Why are you in Virginia?"

"I have family here."

"What part?"

"On the east—you know, near the ocean."

"Oh, nice," said Teresa.

"Do you like the beach?"

"Sometimes. I like the mountains better."

"Aren't you tired of seeing those?" he asked with a hint of sarcasm.

She chuckled. She was a creature of habit. She was comfortable with what was familiar. "How did you end up in Orange?"

"That's where I found work."

"What do you do?"

"I'm a chef."

"Oh, great."

What she would find out later was that Rick worked as a cook on the weekends at a restaurant that served steaks, chicken, and potatoes for the most part, and that his primary source of income was the factory work, just like her.

For now, Teresa was enjoying the conversation. She felt that the two of them were beginning to connect.

Her vulnerability made her feel hopeful. What she didn't know was that Rick was being his slick self. While some bar patrons were good at pool or dancing, Rick was good at getting women into bed. That was his game.

As they were talking, Rick noticed that another man was eyeing Teresa. When he and she weren't talking, he glared at the other man until he made eye contact with Rick. A quick look into Rick's eyes was all it took for the man to not look again.

Back to Teresa, as part of schmoozing her, the next step was to get her to dance.

The couple eventually danced, twice including a slow one to "Penny Lover,"*** which had been popular several years before. During that dance, she could feel the strength in Rick's chest, shoulders, and arms. She liked a strong man. He must work hard for a living. A strong work ethic was one of her must-haves when it came to choosing a partner. After all, that was true of her, and she was known for her perfect attendance at the factory.

They drank a couple of more beers, and then Rick popped the question: "You wanna get out of here?"

Teresa knew what that question meant. It was a lazy way of asking, *Would you like to leave this place and come back to mine?* Either way, the answer would be the same tonight.

"Okay."

*** "Penny Lover" was recorded by Lionel Richie.

Rick smiled. He was about to score again. That's what he did so well. He turned to Teresa and asked, "Care to follow me home?"

"Sure."

The two of them still had their bar tab to pay. Rick motioned for the bartender to come over. "We need to settle up," he said.

The bartender came back a couple of minutes later and directed the bill to Rick. He didn't particularly like spending his own money, but he recognized the importance of making a good impression. The bill was only $8, and he gave the bartender a $10 bill and said, "Keep the change."

Teresa thought maybe Rick was a generous kind of guy. *That's a good thing.*

The two of them walked out of the bar, and Rick asked, "Where are you parked?"

Teresa pointed to her car, and Rick said, "I'll meet you here in a minute."

She got in her car, started the engine, and waited for him.

This second look at his vehicle made her imagination wonder. His was the kind she imagined an elderly man wearing a fedora would drive at forty miles per hour in a 55 mph zone. Funny: she had him pegged as a sports car kind of guy. She thought of the bumper sticker that boasted, "My Other Car Is a Lamborghini."

She reminded herself that it wasn't about the material things. Finding true love was what she wanted.

He motioned for her to follow him, and she did. She noticed there were no bumper stickers on his old beater, which was bluish-gray in color, had four doors, and faded paint. What she didn't know was that quite a few women had discovered just how comfortable and roomy the seats in this car were when engaged in sexual intercourse.

The drive back to his place took them approximately forty-five minutes. He lived in a low-rent duplex in Orange.

He parked parallel with the road in front of his home, and she pulled in behind him. Once inside, it was apparent to her that Rick lived a bachelor's life. She first noticed the kitchen table, which had not been cleaned off. Instead, an empty pizza box and a few beer cans littered it, as well as an ashtray that contained both tobacco and marijuana butts.

In the kitchen, the sink had its share of dirty dishes, and the appliances had their share of grimy fingerprints.

She looked to the living room, where she saw a hodge-podge of furniture. She presumed he had gained such from thrift stores, yard sales, or Goodwill.

A coffee table had its share of dust, and a blanket made a makeshift drapery. Looking out at the rear patio, she noticed the screen door behind the glass door had a hole in it, but since Rick was renting, he probably decided to ignore it.

Truly, Rick was living a bachelor's life.

He invited her to sit down while he went to the refrigerator to retrieve a couple of beers. He asked her if she wanted a glass. Figuring it might not be clean, she said, "No thank you. Just the can or bottle is fine."

Rick preferred Budweiser in a bottle, and he brought two bottles to the living room, where he popped the tops and the two of them slowly sipped them down.

He soon had his arm around her shoulders and she eased into his body. Soon, they kissed passionately.

It felt good to her. Rick, she thought, was a good kisser. Moments later, he asked her if she wanted to get more comfortable and, she whispered yes.

He led her to his bedroom where a nightlight provided the only illumination. They took their clothes off and climbed into bed. Soon they were engaged in some of the most passionate lovemaking she had ever experienced.

She may have been just the next woman on Rick's scorecard, but to her, the sexual intercourse was special. It had been a long time. Despite the fact she regularly went to bars, she hadn't been laid for quite some time, and it felt good.

Rick was good at lovemaking, and she was receptive and reciprocated with equal passion. When it was over, the two of them quickly fell asleep.

Just before Teresa fell asleep, she wondered, *What will he think of me in the morning?*

4

A NEW DAY HAS DAWNED

SHE SLEPT THROUGH the night for the most part. She remembered nothing about her dreams, and when she woke, she looked over at Rick, who was still asleep. Just like last night, she thought he was good-looking.

She moved around a little, and it stirred him from his slumber. He looked over at her with a faint smile.

"Mornin'," he said.

"Good mornin'," she replied.

Ordinarily, after a one-night-stand, he would make up some bogus plan about all the important things he had to do that day to encourage the other party to leave.

Not this time.

"You wanna go out for breakfast?" he asked.

"Sounds good to me."

They got up, put on their clothes, and took turns using the bathroom, where Teresa looked in the mirror and thought, *Not bad.*

Soon they left in his car, and he drove them to the Waffle House. A waitress soon came over to their booth with two mugs and a pot of coffee in her hand. "Coffee?" she asked.

"Yes," they said simultaneously.

As she poured their coffee, the couple perused the menu.

"I'll be back to take your order in a minute," said the waitress, who was missing a front tooth.

After last night's heavy dose of good loving, both had hearty appetites.

"Hey, this is our first breakfast together," said Rick. "I say we get steak and eggs."

"Yeah," said Teresa. "I could eat a horse."

When the waitress returned, Rick said, "Give us two orders of steak and eggs. I'll have toast and hash browns."

"And what about you?" the waitress asked Teresa.

"Toast and grits," she said.

"Okay, thanks. I'll get that order right in."

"Grits?" he asked.

"Yeah, it's a Southern thing."

"Hey, whatever," he said.

The coffee tasted particularly good this morning.

"You know, I really enjoyed last night," said Teresa.

"Me too."

They continued with small talk until the waitress brought their food. After the meal, Rick drove them back to his apartment where, she said she should probably head back home. He walked her to her car.

"I had fun last night," she said.

"Yeah, it was great," replied Rick. "Can I see you again?"

"Sure, give me a call."

"Don't think I have your number."

She reached in her purse and found a small piece of paper and wrote her number on it.

"I'll call you soon," he said.

"Hope so. Don't be a stranger."

She drove off, feeling good.

Today was Saturday, and she had no plans. She would do laundry, maybe catch up with family, or just stay home and watch television. Who knows? Rick might call and she didn't want to be away from home.

Saturday came and went, and she did not hear from Rick, but maybe he was playing it cool. Maybe he didn't want to seem too interested.

Sundays for her were uneventful for the most part. She rarely went to church and often just spent time watching television or spending time with one of her siblings.

Midway through the day, her telephone rang. She felt a few butterflies in her stomach when she considered that the person on the other end may just be Rick.

After two rings she answered.

"Teresa?"

"Yes."

"Hey, it's Rick."

"Hi."

"How's it going?"

"Good. You?"

"Good. Are you busy?"

"Not at all. I was hoping it would be you."

Those words came out too quickly, she thought. She shouldn't sound too eager to hear from him. That could be a strategic mistake.

"Yeah, I was going to call you yesterday, but I figured you were busy. Hey, I was wondering if you'd like to get together next weekend, a friend of mine is having a keg party on Saturday?"

"That sounds great."

"I could pick you up at six."

"I'd like that."

She gave him directions to her home and they hung up. She felt pumped up that she was going to see him again.

The workweek would be a piece of cake knowing she already had plans with Rick for the following weekend. She felt so much excitement that she had a hard time falling asleep on Sunday night.

Still, she felt energized on Monday when she woke up and thought about returning to work at the factory. She showered, brushed her teeth, and grabbed some fruit to eat in the car on her way to work. When she arrived at the factory, she did what was customary; she punched in her time card and reported to her workstation.

She had a visible smile on her face, and one of her coworkers quickly took notice.

"Hey, I know that look, you old hussy," said Tammy.

Teresa smiled and said, "What?"

"I know what *you* did this weekend."

"What are you talking about?"

"You know what I'm talking about. I know that look. You got laid, didn't you?"

Teresa felt a slight blush and then smiled.

"I knew it. You can't fool me. Who's the lucky guy?"

"His name is Rick."

"Rick who?"

"Hmm. Can't say I remember."

"I told you you're an old hussy!"

"Shut up! You're just jealous."

"You're damn right I'm jealous. I'd like to get laid too."

"What's stopping you?" asked Teresa.

"Yeah, easy for you to say. I wouldn't sleep with the guys I meet. They're only interested in one thing."

"Well, not all of them," Teresa said.

"We'll see about that," said Tammy. "You gonna see this guy again?"

"Yes, this weekend."

"Oh, must be serious. You be careful. Don't you let this guy break your heart. If he does, he'll have to answer to me."

"I'm a big girl," said Teresa..

"Yeah, and a happy one today."

The two of them began their tasks, and the day flew by for Teresa. In fact, the whole workweek went by quickly; she was on a high this time, one that was not alcohol or drug induced. Since she had plans with Rick on Saturday, she might just stay at home tonight.

As soon as she started her car's engine, she turned on the radio. After a few commercials, she heard an older song that she had not heard for a long time. It was Johnny Lee's big hit, "Lookin' for Love (in All the Wrong Places)."

For a fleeting moment, she wondered if that song was meant for her. Was the Man up above trying to tell her something? She quickly dismissed the notion and thought about her date with Rick.

This weekend, she would get to know him better.

5

THE COURTSHIP BEGINS

RICK ARRIVED AT her residence right on time. Looking out her window, she saw him in a different vehicle. She soon learned that his Ford pickup truck was his preferred vehicle of choice.

She greeted him at the door with a smile, a hug, and a kiss.

"Ready to go?" he asked.

"Yes."

With a noticeably puzzled look on his face, she asked him, "Is anything wrong?"

"No. Why?"

"I was trying to figure out why you were looking at me kind of funny."

"Actually," he said, "your eyes look different today. in a good way. Last night when we met, I thought they were brown. Today they actually look green."

She laughed. "They do change color. Depends on what kind of mood I'm in, or maybe what I'm wearing."

"What kind of mood are you in?"

"A good one."

He opened the passenger door for her. Once he was behind the wheel, she asked, "A pickup truck, huh?"

"Yeah, there's something about a truck. I'd much rather drive it than anything else."

"So who is your friend?" she asked.

"Someone I met through work. His name is Randall."

"By the way," she said, "this seems kind of dumb, but I don't remember your last name."

"I'm not sure I ever said."

"Well, what is it?'

"My last name is *Koenig*."

"That's not the kind of name we hear in Madison," she said.

"Well, I did tell you I was born in New York."

"Oh yes, Yankee by birth."

"Yeah, but remember, my family moved to Florida when I was three."

"Yeah, but when did you come to Virginia?"

"I came to Orange in 1986."

"Hmm." She did the math in her head and thought, *That was six years ago.*

"So what have you been doing all this time?

"Working, mostly. I mentioned that I'm a chef, and I also have a job at a factory in Gordonsville. I plan to start my own handyman service one day."

"So what about your parents?"

"What about them?"

"Are they still around?"

"My mom is living in Florida."

"What about your dad?"

"I don't like to talk about him."

"I don't like to talk about mine much either," said Teresa. "My daddy is an alcoholic and is mean to my momma."

"Well, at least you have a dad," said Rick. "Mine was never around."

"Your poor mom must have had it hard."

"My mom looked out for us and worked jobs many people wouldn't work."

"Do you mind me asking like what?"

"She worked at hotels, cleaning. I remember she was an alcoholic and drug user, and we had to move around a lot. Hell, we spent most of the time living in motels and trailer parks."

"That sucks," she said.

"Well, we all have our stories to tell. What about you?"

"I'm from Madison. I come from a large family. Momma looked out for us. Daddy was either too drunk or too busy chasing other women to do us much good. I hated it when he was home. If it hadn't been for my momma I don't know what we would have done."

"Looks like you turned out all right," he said.

"Thanks."

She eased her way a little closer to him. There was obvious sexual chemistry between them. He put his arm around her, and she put her hand on his thigh. A few minutes later, they reached their destination.

Randall's home was located down a long stretch of back road in Orange County. It was Memorial Day weekend, and parties and cookouts were prevalent.

As soon as they pulled into the driveway Teresa noticed a number of people who appeared to be already drunk.

Allen recognized Rick and his truck, so he approached the vehicle. "Hey Rick! Thanks for coming."

"We wouldn't want to miss it."

"We?"

"Yeah, this is Teresa."

"Hey Teresa."

"Hi."

"Hey, make yourself at home. There's cold beer on tap, and Joel is cooking up hot dogs, hamburgers, and chicken. We got horseshoes and a volleyball net set up."

Rick went over to the keg, and a guy offered to pour him a cup of beer.

"Can you make it two?" asked Rick. "One for the lady." He motioned toward Teresa.

"Sure thing."

Rick took the two cups of beer and gave one to her.

They began to mingle among the crowd.

From a distance, Teresa spotted someone she thought she knew from work. "I think I know that girl," she said to Rick.

"Why don't you go find out? I'll wait for you here."

Teresa walked toward the girl; and one of Rick's friends, Tim, walked up to him.

"What's up, you old snake?" asked Tim.

"Same old shit man."

"Who's the new lady?"

"Her name is Teresa."

"Your latest conquest I guess?"

"Not really. There's something about her that's different."

"Yeah, we'll see about that, you stud. You're always dipping your wick in something new. How's about we twist one up when we get a chance?"

"Sounds good to me," said Rick.

"Does she smoke?"

"Yeah."

"That's cool."

"How is she in bed?"

"Like you wouldn't believe," replied Rick.

"No wonder you're keeping her around."

"We have some things in common."

"I hope she's not too much like you," said Tim.

"Hey, let's talk later. She's coming back this way," said Rick. "I might want to throw a few horseshoes and suck down some suds before we burn one."

"You got it."

Teresa approached Rick, who handed her a beer. She said, "That girl works at the same place as me, just a different shift. I knew I had seen her before."

"You wanna throw some horseshoes?" he asked.

"Sure, why not."

After a few minutes of this, Rick got bored and suggested they smoke a joint. Allen had a shed on the property where he rolled a many of them.

Rick and Teresa ventured that way, where they saw Randall holding in the smoke from the toke he had just taken. He motioned for them to come in. Randall was there with a couple of other guys, and the joint went around. A few tokes later, Rick and Teresa headed back for another beer.

They walked by a couple of women who nodded and smiled at Rick. Intuitively, Teresa thought they may have been intimate with him at one time or another, or maybe the weed she had just smoked made her feel a little paranoid. She reminded herself not to dwell on anything negative. Instead, enjoy the party. And enjoy Rick.

Horseshoes, beer, weed, grilled chicken and burgers, and a try at volleyball consumed the rest of the day for Rick and Teresa. As darkness approached, they decided to go home. Rick was obviously under the influence but assured Teresa he could drive just fine. He drove them back to his place, where she spent the night.

The couple spent a quiet Sunday together, and then it was back to work for both of them the next day.

Teresa had already decided that she was content to date Rick exclusively. She liked him. There was tremendous chemistry between them, and they were touchy-feely. She assumed he felt the same for her. For a period of time, there was no reason to think otherwise.

The summer and fall months passed with the two of them in a steady relationship that looked promising to all who saw them together. Glaringly absent from the view was both his and her family members.

Rick balked at the notion that Teresa should meet his family. They were weird. He was much more receptive to meeting her family. As the holidays approached, Teresa decided she would introduce Rick to her mother and siblings. In advance of Christmas, she told Jenny that she was dating someone and she wanted her to meet him.

The plan was set: Teresa would bring Rick to the family Christmas gathering.

The year was 1992.

The sibling whose turn it was to host this year's holiday gathering was younger sister Lori.

On Christmas Day, Rick picked up Teresa and drove them to Lori's home in Madison County. Lori was married and had two small children. Her husband, Randy, worked as a logger and helped build their home nestled in a wooded area. There was some seclusion to their home, and the property featured a small creek.

One of Randy's favorite hobbies was to ride four-wheelers, and this location suited him fine.

A large field separated two stretches of woods.

Traditionally, the entire Dodson family—minus the father who in time was divorced from the mother or simply away from family pursuing other women—assembled, brought a dish to share, sang Christmas carols, and exchanged gifts. There was always homemade eggnog and boiled custard, plus candies and other assorted goodies. A wood stove provided the primary source of heat, and the smell of it was always a reminder of home.

The men of the family wore jeans, flannel shirts, and baseball caps; drank beer; dipped or smoked tobacco; and talked about women, NASCAR, hunting, fishing, and more about women.

The women of this family were modest, dressed casually, and all contributed to the warmth of the celebration. But they were not women who could be trampled. Teresa wasn't the only one known for speaking her mind. She reserved that right, and so did her sisters.

The matriarch, of course, was Martha Dodson, the woman with a saintly reputation for devotion to family, hard work, and going above and beyond to look out for others.

She had done her part to raise the children—five daughters and three sons—and to make them feel safe. Of course, there were emotional ramifications as a result of having a father who had done them all a terrible injustice with his abuse and hard drinking.

Martha hoped her children would choose well when it came to life partners. Though Teresa was the third of her eight children, she had not yet married, and the breakup she went through with her high school boyfriend dealt her an emotional setback to which Martha was well attuned.

But Martha had heard that her daughter had met someone and was especially eager to meet her suitor. Knowing the hurt and loss Teresa had previously suffered, Martha would look kindly on her new beau.

For Teresa, she desired affirmation from her family about Rick. She wanted to know that her mother and siblings, especially Jenny, liked him. Teresa was considerably older than Jenny, but the two of them had grown close in recent years, and Teresa planned to ask Jenny directly what she thought of Rick. She knew Jenny would be honest.

When Rick and Teresa arrived at Lori's, the driveway was full, and they parked in the grass. Soon, Lori opened the side door and greeted them.

"Merry Christmas!" she said. "Come on in. We've been waiting for you."

Rick and Teresa walked in the door, and Teresa introduced him to Lori.

"Nice to meet you," said Lori.

"Nice to meet you too," he said.

"Come inside. How's my big sister?"

"Good. How are you? And thanks for having us."

Inside, Rick and Teresa soon found themselves the center of attention as all eyes were focused on them. In the middle of the assembly was Martha, who smiled, walked toward her beloved daughter, hugged her, and said, "Merry Christmas. I love you so much."

"Merry Christmas, Momma," said Teresa. "I want you to meet Rick. Rick, this is my mom."

Rick and Martha exchanged pleasantries, and then Teresa took turns introducing Rick to everyone else.

Off in a corner stood an ever-vigilant Jenny, who was taking it all in and processing the information in her brain.

She learned a long time ago she could trust her intuition. It was a gift from God. And she trusted God.

Teresa's mother and sisters did their part to make Rick feel at home. Teresa's brothers were civil and reserved. Martha, always loyal to her children, took the opportunity to engage with Rick.

"Rick, we know so little about you."

"I've been around here about six years," he said.

"Where are you from?"

"I grew up in Florida."

"What do you do for a living?"

"I'm a chef for the most part."

"Where at?"

"Over at Clyde's Family Restaurant in Orange."

"What do you like to cook?"

"The usual American cuisine: steak, chicken, potatoes, gravy, you name it."

"Did you go to culinary school?"

"Oh no," said Rick. "I was always a natural at cooking. It's just one of the things that I do. When I was in school, I was a good athlete, if I say so myself, and could have played football in college. A number of Division I schools were interested in me. I turned them down."

"Were you also a good student?"

"Yes, I was. I was an honor roll student, and sometimes made Dean's List. I was named 'Who's Who Among

American High School Students.' I did really good. My coaches liked me; my teachers liked me; I had a lot of friends. I had a chance to play football in college."

'And a big head,' thought Martha.

"So do you think you'll stay at the restaurant for awhile longer?" asked Martha.

"For the time," he said. "But I also have a job at a factory and I plan to start my own business as a handy man. I know some guys that want to work for me. They all look up to me. I can do just about anything you can think of. If I can't do it, it probably can't be done."

One of Martha's sons, Doug, looked over at Rick, and the two of them had a momentary staredown.

Martha sensed the friction and redirected Rick to the living room, where the rest of the family was gathered.

Overall, the gathering went well. No one drank too much. No one argued. No one called the police. No one wanted to punch Rick, not even Doug, yet; and when it was over, the siblings hugged each other and their mother and wished each other a Merry Christmas.

Rick and Teresa left and headed back to his house. They would enjoy their first Christmas together. Their lovemaking would be extra special.

On their way to Rick's house Teresa said, "I think you made a good impression."

Rick smiled smugly and thought, *Who wouldn't like me?*

Tomorrow, Teresa would call Jenny to find out what she thought.

Jenny would like Rick. Teresa did.

Back at Lori's home, Rick was the talk of the night.

6

HAVE YOUR WAY

CHRISTMAS DAY 1992 fell on a Friday. The factory was closed on the weekends, so Teresa could enjoy the time off; but the restaurant that employed Rick was open for business the day after Christmas, and he was due to go in at 10:30 a.m.

After he left for work, Teresa drove home and showered. After a bite to eat, she called Jenny. She answered on the third ring.

"Hey, it's Teresa."

"Hey, what are you doing?"

"Just got up a little while ago and figuring out what to do today."

Jenny paused in silence.

"Well?" asked Teresa.

"Well what?"

"You know what I'm talking about," said Teresa. "What did you think?"

Jenny paused again. "You know that we all want you to be happy," she said.

"Well, no shit. I know that. What did you think of Rick?"

"I have to tell you," said Jenny, "I didn't get a good vibe about him."

"What do you mean?"

"I just don't feel good about him."

"Well, I like him," said Teresa.

"And I want you to be happy," replied Jenny. "What do you know about his family?"

"Why is that so important? I'm not in a relationship with his family; I'm in a relationship with him."

"Don't you think it's a little weird that y'all have been dating for several months and you don't know anything about his family? Have you even met them?"

"No," said Teresa. "He doesn't talk about his father, and his mother lives in Florida. Besides, Rick and I are serious about each other."

"You don't know enough about him to get serious."

"Sorry I asked."

"Maybe we…" Jenny was unable to finish her sentence. Teresa had hung up.

Jenny was disappointed that the conversation ended under such circumstances, but neither she nor Teresa would ever lie. Their mother always taught them to tell the truth; it was the right thing to do.

For now, Jenny decided to give Teresa space and let her think about it. Nothing Teresa could do would ever change the love Jenny felt for her. But she had asked, so Jenny answered. No apology from Jenny would follow.

About an hour later, Teresa telephoned again. "Hey, it's me. I'm sorry for hanging up on you."

"It's okay. I understand."

"You have to know how hurt I was when my first boy-friend broke up with me. Remember, I found out he was interested in another guy?"

"Yes," said Jenny. "We all hurt for you."

"And now that I've found someone, I just want my family to like him."

"I wouldn't have told you what I did if I didn't love you," said Jenny. "There's nothing I want more than for my big sister to be happy."

"I know."

"And who knows? Maybe I'm wrong about him and we'll all come to like him," said Jenny.

"I hope so," replied Teresa. "Anyway, what are you doing today?"

"Going to Momma's. You wanna come over?"

"Yeah, I think I should. Rick is at work, and I'm alone. I'll meet you over there in about an hour."

"Okay, see you then."

Jenny called their mother to let her know that she and Teresa would be coming over.

When Teresa arrived at her mother's, Jenny was already there, and she recognized the pickup truck belonging to the youngest of her three brothers, Billy Lee, in the driveway.

Teresa entered through the side door and saw the three of them sitting at the kitchen table drinking tea or coffee.

"How y'all doing?" asked Teresa.

"Good to see you again so soon," said her mother.

Jenny came over and hugged Teresa. Billy Lee sat in the chair and watched.

Though Billy Lee was the youngest of the three boys, he was arguably the most protective of his sisters. Last night, he and Rick talked little, but Billy Lee observed much. He had a reputation for having a short fuse and some calloused fists. He brought a load of firewood to his mother this day, and when he heard that his sisters were coming over, he decided to stay.

"I'm glad we were able to get together for Christmas," said Martha.

"It's always good to be back home, Momma," said Teresa.

Martha heated up some of yesterday's leftovers and had the table set for four.

Teresa knew how Jenny felt about Rick but she had not yet heard from her mother, or her brother.

"Momma, what did you think of Rick?"

"You wanna know the truth? I think you better be real careful. Don't you let him take advantage of you. I gotta feeling he's all about himself."

"And he's right much of a smart aleck," Billy Lee chimed in. "He thinks a whole lot of himself. I'd say he's got a lot more mouth than he's got ass."

"Let's try to enjoy our family time," said Martha.

"I hate it that y'all think like that," said Teresa. "I'm gone." She bolted to the door, and no one tried to stop her.

Inside, the three of them heard Teresa slam her car door shut and accelerate out of the driveway. She would not be heard from for a while. She had made her decision about Rick, and though she would have liked the affirmation from her family, she would chalk that up as the way it was and go on about her business.

Teresa and Rick were in a relationship. People would just have to get used to it.

She returned home and enjoyed a few beers. She would take it easy the rest of the weekend and get ready for the workweek. She and Rick would see each other before then. She hoped he wouldn't ask about her family. If he did, she would think of something to say.

Then it occurred to her that maybe she should meet his family. She had asked before. He had balked at the idea. Maybe now would be a better time.

One thing she knew for certain: she and Rick would have things their way.

In time, both families would be on board. Or at least she thought.

7

THE BEST OF ALL OPTIONS?

AFTER TERESA'S ABRUPT exit from her mother's house, she had no contact with her family the next day. A quiet Sunday passed, and it was back to work on Monday. The job at the factory would keep her busy and her mind off the disappointment. She felt that her family did not like Rick.

When she arrived at work, the place was quiet. After all, who wanted to come back to work after a holiday?

Her first encounter was with Tammy.

"How was Christmas?" Tammy asked.

"It was all right," replied Teresa.

"Just all right?"

"Yeah, just all right. What about you?"

"It was good. We all got together, and nobody called the cops," she said with a laugh.

"Well, they say you can pick your friends and your nose, but you can't pick your family," said Teresa.

"Something tells me that means something," said Tammy.

"Yeah, my family doesn't like Rick."

"Well, that's too bad," said Tammy. "But maybe they'll change."

"No," said Teresa. "They don't change. Damn it to hell."

"Whoa," said Tammy. "Must be bad for you to use words like that. That's not you."

"It is today," snapped Teresa.

"Let's get to work before the boss man sees us," said Tammy.

They went to work and when five o'clock rolled around, they punched in their time cards and said good-bye.

Once home, Teresa called Rick to see how his day went. They decided to go out to a local bar for some drinks and dinner. That night, they talked about their relationship and where it might be headed.

Teresa took the lead. "So what do you think?"

"What do I think about what?" he said.

"What do you think about us?"

"I think us is a good thing."

"You know what I mean."

"Well, like what exactly do you mean?"

"Are we going to date just each other?"

"Yeah, sure. If that's what you want."

"Isn't that what you want?" she pressed.

"Sure, I'm cool with that," he said.

To a certain extent now, she felt as though things were official between her and Rick.

When it came down to it, she considered herself a one-man woman. She assumed and hoped that Rick was a one-woman man. At this point in time, she had no reason to think otherwise.

When the evening was over the two of them went to Rick's for a while, and then she returned home to get ready for another day at work. She looked forward to telling Tammy the good news that she and Rick were now going together.

Deep down, she wished Rick had been more enthusiastic about their relationship, but she reminded herself that guys often didn't share their feelings. They expressed themselves differently.

She went into work the next day and immediately looked for Tammy. "Good morning."

"Good morning," said Tammy. "You've got something on your mind again."

"Yeah," said Teresa. "I talked to Rick last night. We are a couple. We just want to date each other.

"Congratulations," said Tammy. "I hope it's everything you want it to be. You are a good friend. You've been through a lot. You deserve the best, girl."

"Thank you. Guess we'd better get to work."

"The playoffs start this weekend," said Tammy.

"Yeah, Redskins and Cowboys both made it," said Teresa. "They don't play each other yet."

"If they do, that's kind of like you against me," said Tammy good-naturedly.

"Yeah, we'd probably go at it if we watched the game in the same room," quipped Teresa.

"Does Rick like football?" asked Tammy.

"I think so. We haven't really talked about football. He was born in New York and grew up in Florida, so he may not like the Redskins or the Cowboys. I'll have to ask him soon. He said he played football in high school and was good enough to play in college."

"Did he?"

"No, he decided not to."

"Hmm," said Tammy.

Teresa and Tammy both loved football. Teresa and her family were Redskins fans. Tammy and hers were Cowboys fans. The friendly banter between them was a good thing. Teresa questioned why anyone from Virginia would like the Cowboys when the Redskins were considered local. Tammy usually countered with the reminder that the Cowboys had fans all over the world, including Washington, DC. This usually left Teresa uncharacteristically speechless, but only for a moment. Teresa ordinarily had something to say.

About a week later, Rick invited Teresa to have dinner at Clyde's Family Restaurant where she could enjoy some of his cooking, of which he was so proud.

He told her to come to the restaurant on Saturday around 6:00 p.m., and he would prepare her meal.

She was delighted to enjoy the opportunity. This would be part of the getting-to-know-him-better process. What a change in the traditional roles for which she was accustomed. Her father never cooked for the family. Her mother did that—and just about everything else. Having a man who could cook would be a plus.

Rather than being a few minutes fashionably late, as she had been coached by one of her sisters to do, she did the opposite: she came a few minutes early. She approached the entrance with a broad smile on her face, but as she walked in, she saw Rick acting flirtatiously with another customer. Both of them were obviously enjoying their conversation. The customer reciprocated with her own flirting—the batting of the eyelashes, the body language, the warm smile, to name a few. Teresa's countenance quickly changed. She almost bolted out of the restaurant. Instead, she paused momentarily and stood still. Rick happened to see her peripherally and quickly looked up, straightened up, and blush.

The customer continued to smile until she looked back toward Teresa, whose piercing eyes stopped her cold.

Teresa then approached Rick, who directed her gently to a booth. Knowing she was unhappy, he went out of his way to be a gentleman. The damage, to some extent, was done. She would not forget the moment, but she would forgive him because she was interested in their relationship lasting and being a success.

"Glad you're here," said Rick.

"Hope I'm not interrupting anything," she said.

"Of course not: I was just doing a little PR work with our customers."

"You picked a good-looking woman to do your PR work on."

"That was it and nothing more," said Rick. "I think you'll like the food. I'm planning on cooking a steak for you. How do you like it cooked?"

"Well done. You can just about burn it."

"I'll make it with mashed potatoes, gravy, and green beans," said Rick. "The waitress will be over to take your drink order."

By now, the customer with whom Rick had been talking decided to pay her bill and leave. After paying at the register, she walked by Teresa, but did not attempt to make eye contact.

Soon a waitress came over and took Teresa's drink order.

"I'll have sweet tea," she said.

"Did Rick take your food order?"

"Yes."

Teresa thought about Rick's flirtatious behavior but then reminded herself that most guys were flirts, especially those who were good looking. And Rick was good-looking.

She reasoned that as their relationship grew his tendency to flirt would lessen because he would be happy with her. They were a good match, had much in common, and the sexual chemistry was tremendous.

The waitress brought both drink and dinner to her, and she looked over at Rick who was behind the window to the kitchen, and the two of them nodded as if he was saying, *Enjoy.*

As Teresa was eating, she noticed a man had come into the restaurant and approached the area usually reserved for employees and engaged Rick in conversation. As she watched, she noticed that Rick handed this man a sum of money.

Hmm, she thought. *A debt? A loan? A bet? Never mind. Not my business.*

After the meal, Rick told her to enjoy the evening and he would see her tomorrow.

Tomorrow meant Sunday, and this time of year meant football and the playoffs.

"I know you like football," said Teresa. "Would you like to watch the game tomorrow?"

"Who's playing?" asked Rick.

"The Redskins."

"Anybody else?"

"Does that mean you don't like the Redskins?"

"Actually, I'm a Dolphins fan," said Rick. "They won their division."

"The Redskins are a wild card team. They play Minnesota. Well, you don't have to pull for the Redskins. Just as long as you're not a Dallas fan."

"No," said Rick. "Really just the Dolphins."

He knew enough about the game and the playoffs to know that those two teams would not be matched up unless both made it to the Super Bowl.

"The game starts at one," said Teresa. "Come over to my place before that and I'll fix lunch and we'll watch the game."

"Sounds good," replied Rick. "I'll see you then."

The couple kissed, and she drove home. Rick went back to work. He still had about three hours before closing.

At 10:00 p.m., he had cooked the last order and had begun the cleanup of the kitchen. Soon, he would rendezvous with another lady—the same lady Teresa had seen him talking to when she arrived at the restaurant. The two of them had made plans to get together when Rick got off work. They had finalized their plans before Teresa walked into the place.

When he got off work, Rick drove south to a bar to meet the lucky new lady on his list.

The two of them met up as planned, shared a few drinks, danced a little, and then went back to Rick's place for the night. She would need to leave early in the morning. Rick would see to that. He needed to get cleaned up and stop by a convenience store before arriving at Teresa's.

Rick and the lucky lady enjoyed a night of long sex. In the morning, Rick expressed his customary desire to see the person again but said he had a number of things to attend to, which implied it was time for her to leave. Though it was Sunday, church was never on his list of things to do.

His latest conquest complied and left his place. Rick fixed something to eat, and then showered and watched television for a while.

At about 11:00 a.m., he left his house to see Teresa. On his way, he stopped at 7-Eleven and purchased a lottery ticket. One day he would hit it and make it big.

This, like every other time before it, was not the day. "Easy come, easy go," he said to himself. That was his philosophy with the lottery and with women. To him, the two had much in common.

He arrived at Teresa's, where she met him at the door with a kiss.

"How did the rest of work go for you last night?" she asked.

"It went good," he said. "Just another night on the job."

"Get comfortable," she said. "The game comes on at one. I'll fix us something to eat."

When that time came, she tuned the station to the play-off game between her beloved Redskins and the Minnesota Vikings. She cheered when her team played well and yelled a few obscenities when they didn't. Rick watched quietly, not emotionally connected to either team.

When it was over, the Redskins had won and earned the right to advance to next week's game against the San Francisco 49ers.

No need to turn to the other channel: Rick's Dolphins had a first-round bye and would not play until next week.

Over the course of the next couple of weeks, they tuned in every Sunday for the playoff games. Her Redskins lost to the 49ers in the Division Championship round, and then the 49ers lost to the Dallas Cowboys in the NFC title game.

Rick's Dolphins lost to the Buffalo Bills, which won the AFC.

In this year's Super Bowl, the Bills and the Cowboys would meet.

She would have to pull for the Bills.

Each year, one of her family members hosted a Super Bowl party, and this year it was the turn of her oldest sibling, Annette. Not only did family members show up, but so did friends and coworkers. She contacted Annette before the Super Bowl party and told her she would be there, along with Rick.

When Rick and Teresa arrived at Annette's, the house was already full of family and friends.

Teresa reacquainted Rick with the family members he had met at the Christmas party and introduced him to some extended family members and friends he had not met. Annette had a couple of coworkers in attendance, Connie and Emily.

The Super Bowl party was much more fun than the game, which turned out to be a blowout in favor of the Cowboys. Rick drank his share of beer and toward the end of the party, began to slur his words.

Teresa also drank, but not in excess. She offered to drive them home, but Rick wouldn't let her.

Rick took her home, where they kissed good night and said they would talk tomorrow. The next day was Monday, and it was back to work at the factory for both of them.

Later during the week, they talked about their plans for the upcoming weekend. Teresa had a family get-together planned for Saturday and invited Rick, who declined, saying he was going out of town to visit his sister. That was a lie.

On Saturday, he went to his favorite watering hole looking for a one-night-stand. At the Oasis, he mingled for a period of time and made incidental eye contact with a woman he thought looked familiar. The two of them did not talk. This lady's name was Connie, a friend of Annette's who was at the Super Bowl party.

Rick then danced with another customer, and soon the two of them were talking intimately and eventually left the bar together and headed to his place. The next day, Connie telephoned Annette.

"Hey, this is Connie. Watcha doin'?"

"Hey, just got back from church and getting lunch ready for the kids. You?"

"Not much. Hey, I was at the Oasis last night and saw a guy I think is the one that Teresa is dating. I'm pretty sure it was him. And he wasn't there with Teresa. He left with another woman."

"Oh shit," said Annette. "You know, my mom and our family don't like him. I haven't said anything to Teresa, but I don't want her to get used or be hurt again."

"Are you going to tell her?" asked Connie.

"Yes, I think I should."

"Okay. I'll see you at work this week," Connie said.

"Thanks for letting me know."

"Hate to be the bearer of bad news. See you later."

Later in the day, Annette called Teresa.

"Hey, it's Annette."

"Hey, how's it going?"

"Fine. You?"

"Good. What's up?"

"Listen, I don't mean to upset you, but Connie told me she saw Rick at the Oasis the other night with another woman. She said the two of them left together."

"Damn," said Teresa. "He told me he was going out of town to see his sister."

"Sorry. I hated to have to break this to you, but no one wants you to get hurt."

"Thanks, Annette. Guess I'll take this up with Rick."

"Hope it goes well. Come see us again soon."

"Okay."

Teresa seethed for a while, and then she called Rick. When he answered, she asked him how the weekend went.

"Pretty good," he said. "What about you?"

"It was all right. How is your sister?"

"She's fine."

"How was the trip?"

"Long and boring," said Rick.

"Anything else?" she asked.

"What do you mean? Like what?"

"Rick, Annette's friend saw you with another woman at the Oasis, and that you left with her."

"Who told you that?"

"Never mind who. Did you?"

Rick hesitated and then said, "I went by there for a beer."

"What about the other woman?"

"We talked, and then we went outside and got high. That's all."

"Rick, I need to think about this. Maybe we shouldn't see each other for a while. I don't want to get hurt again. I have to know I can trust you."Teresa hung up the phone and cried.

The next day at work, she was noticeably unhappy. She told Tammy, who counseled her to break up with Rick and offered to punch Rick in the face.

Teresa declined her offer. Instead, she would simply not see him for a while and decide later if she should take him back.

In time, she did take Rick back. She loved him and had proven willing to forgive him for any improprieties. Her family never affirmed the relationship, but that did not deter her from continuing it.

In the early part of 1993, the couple was back together and enjoying each other in every way. Her parents had divorced, but her father had quit drinking and he and Teresa had reconciled as much as was possible.

Teresa's family saw her and Rick together at an occasional family function. It was clear to everyone that Teresa had chosen Rick, and she would not be dissuaded.

Both of them continued to work at their jobs at the factory, and he continued to work as a chef on the weekends. He told her and her family that he also planned on starting his own handyman business to generate some additional income.

All appeared to be going well for Teresa, including her perfect attendance at work.

Then one day, sickness almost interrupted the streak. And this time, it was a sickness she had never felt before.

The night before, she had felt dizzy on her feet and a little nauseated. She drank some ginger ale and went to sleep, hoping to feel better in the morning.

When she woke, she still felt nauseous and almost fainted. She tried to shrug it off and went to work.

Tammy met her first thing and said, "You don't look so good."

"Thanks a lot," replied Teresa.

"No, I mean really. You don't look so good. I'm concerned. Are you okay?"

"I've been feeling like I'm going to puke," said Teresa. "I even thought I was going to pass out this morning when I was in the bathroom. I feel like I could heave now."

"Oh my God," exclaimed Tammy. "Are you pregnant?

"Pregnant? God, I hope not."

"Are you using birth control?"

"No."

"Well, why the hell not?"

"I don't feel like talking about this now."

"I think you need to go to the doctor," said Tammy. "You might be pregnant."

Teresa, with the aid of some ginger ale and crackers, managed to get through the day. Before that, she called her doctor's office on her lunch break and scheduled an appointment.

The doctor could see her the next day at four thirty. She approached her employer, who told her to leave early to get to her appointment on time.

The next day, she worked up until three thirty and then drove to her doctor's office where her longtime family doctor had the nurse administer a pregnancy test on her. Sure enough, she was pregnant.

This changed things. She immediately began to wonder what Rick's reaction would be. He didn't seem ready to be a father, and she hadn't planned on being a mother outside of wedlock.

That night, she called Rick and told him the news.

At the mention of her pregnancy, he said nothing. She knew his silence was not a good thing. But she recognized he was as surprised as she.

The couple stayed together, and Rick said nothing for a while about marriage. But when she told the news of her pregnancy to her family, the consensus was unanimous: Rick would need to do the honorable thing and marry her.

Though they did not like him, they liked the idea of abortion or single parenting even less.

Should Rick balk at the idea, a shotgun wedding would be in order.

Teresa told Rick how her family felt, and eight months into her pregnancy, he relented. He would marry her at the place of her choosing.

Teresa, with the input from her family, chose a place in Madison. The structure was not a church but, rather, a meeting hall of sorts where different functions took place.

The date chosen was March 30, 1993.

Rather than calling upon the services of a pastor, they opted to have the ceremony performed by a justice of the peace, who happened to be Teresa's boss at the factory.

Like many days during any early spring in Virginia, this day was cold and rainy.

Jenny remembered to this day how freezing cold it felt.

There were no bridesmaids or groomsmen. Teresa's family, including her father, all came. No one from Rick's family came. Their absence felt as chilly as the weather.

As Rick gazed around at the crowd, he felt that he was part of a shotgun wedding, which could have taken place literally had any of Teresa's brothers gone to their trucks to retrieve their guns.

That wasn't necessary today. Rick said, "I do."

It was official: Teresa and Rick were married.

In less than two months, she would give birth to their first child.

8

MARRIAGE
(MINUS THE BLISS)

THE NEWLYWEDS TOOK up residence at the house Teresa had inherited from her grandmother.

Teresa's grandma knew her granddaughter would take care of the home. She knew of Teresa's solid work ethic and her fiscal responsibility. Her only concern had been Teresa's drinking, but had she been alive at the time Teresa was married, she would have been relieved to know that she had significantly cut back on her consumption of alcohol, especially since she was pregnant.

In preparation for her expected delivery, Teresa enlisted the support of her siblings for the furnishings she would need for the baby. Thanks to ultrasound technology, Teresa and Rick expected to be parents of a baby boy. Not knowing if this baby would be their last, they agreed that the child would be named after him.

With a home already paid for, coupled with their combined incomes, they should have no problem managing their finances and providing well for any children they might have.

Teresa had worked hard and managed to save some money. She knew little about Rick's financial situation other than the fact that he had two jobs and hoped to add a third. He drove an old beater of a car but also had a truck that he preferred and which would be used as a work vehicle in the future.

She assumed the role of the financier in their family and made sure the bills were paid. He agreed to give her a portion of his earnings to assist in the process.

In May of 1993, Teresa gave birth to a son. They immediately decided to call him Little Ricky.

Teresa spent the next six weeks on maternity leave and took good care of the baby. She liked being a mother, and anyone who saw her with her child immediately thought she was a good mom. She rarely drank alcohol, and the use of illegal drugs was definitely a thing of the past. She decided early on to be a devoted mother. Like many parents, she would have been willing to lay down her life for any of her children.

During those six weeks, she also prepared dinner for her husband, who continued to work at the factory during the week and at the restaurant on weekends.

Before the six weeks were up, she contacted one of her great-aunts, Doris, and asked her if she was willing to babysit Little Ricky. Doris quickly agreed, and Teresa paid her a weekly rate for her services.

As for Rick, he no doubt loved his son, but his interaction with him was limited. He did not like the changing of diapers and the crying at night. He figured he would have better interaction with his son when he got older. Then, too, Rick had not grown up in an intact household. His father had been absent most of the time, and his mother had changed jobs frequently and moved the children around a lot. Lessons on stability, dependability, and constancy had not been learned.

And Rick never did cut back on his drinking. He often came home late from work with a heavy odor of alcohol on his breath and would often fall asleep on the couch with the television on. Several times, Teresa would wake up at night, turn the television off, and encourage him to come to bed.

Worse still, she had heard the rumors of Rick chasing other women. She remembered her first visit to the restaurant, where she found him flirting with one of the customers. She hoped that his change in marital status would bring about a change in this behavior. If the rumors were true, then he had not changed, and their marriage would not be a happy one.

Though Rick had done the honorable thing by marrying her, none of her family members liked him, so she limited the contact she and Rick had with her family. There were the annual family picnics and Christmas celebrations, but little else. Each time Rick came with her, the consensus was the same: he was arrogant and full of himself. When seen in public, he was often flirtatious.

But to her, Rick was not only her husband but also the father of her child. With or without her family's blessings, she would do her best to make the marriage work. She held out hope that in time, he would mature and be a devoted husband and father.

When they had free time, the couple made trips to Charles Town, West Virginia, for the horse races, where Rick enjoyed betting on horses, and drinking. They also went to Florida when the opportunity arose because Rick's mother still lived there, and he loved her and the beach.

The trips to Florida made Teresa feel uncomfortable. It was odd enough that none of Rick's family attended their wedding, it was odder still the feeling Teresa had whenever she was in his mother's home. Rick's mother, Dorothy Koenig, had struggled for most of her life. She had been a single parent trying to raise her children. And she struggled with her addiction to alcohol. She likely had undiagnosed mental health issues as well. As adults, her children were always in trouble. How could she ever know peace?

Teresa felt sympathy for her mother-in-law, but not for her two sisters-in-law who seemed to always be at the home whenever she and Rick visited. In her own simple expression, she concluded that the two sisters simply gave her the creeps.

While she certainly did not count herself as a very spiritual person, she concluded that Rick and his family had even less spirituality and flat out did not believe in God.

Perhaps the most defining moment in her experiences with her in-laws came the first time she made the visit.

She and Rick had arranged to be off from work for a few days, and they drove in her car to Florida to visit his family. It was a long trip made longer by the frequent stops made necessary by having a small child.

When they arrived, Dorothy greeted them at the door and welcomed them into her home. Dorothy first hugged Rick and then Teresa.

"It's nice to have you here," she told Teresa.

"It's nice to finally meet you," Teresa replied.

"Come. Let me show you the room you will stay in."

Before they reached the room, Rick's oldest sister, Crystal, came into their presence. Immediately, Teresa felt a cold chill.

Crystal and Teresa looked each other in the eyes. Though Crystal smiled, Teresa did not sense any kindness. Instead, she sensed darkness. And though Crystal wore plenty of makeup, it did little to alter her countenance.

After an exchange of pleasantries, Dorothy showed Rick and Teresa to their room, where they placed their luggage and then joined Dorothy and Crystal for refreshments in the kitchen.

Teresa gazed around at the knickknacks on the refrigerator, the decorations on the wall, and any family photos that might be available in an attempt to understand her in-laws.

She reasoned that this was a blue-collar family of limited formal education and that the family had difficulty hiding its sadness. Something was missing, but she could not pinpoint exactly what.

In the pictures, everyone was smiling, but no one seemed genuinely happy.

On the refrigerator were small magnets that indicated personal preferences for the American and Confederate flags, for Harley-Davidson motorcycles, and for the National Football League.

Knowing that Rick was a Dolphins fan and that they were in Dolphins country, she presumed she was one Redskin among several Dolphins fans. If that was the worst thing she would experience on this trip, things wouldn't be so bad.

But it wasn't the worst thing she experienced.

That night, when it was time to turn in and get some sleep, she and Rick lay down on the bed; but before turning out the light, she caught a glimpse of something that immediately aroused her curiosity. She looked for a closer inspection. She soon discovered that a number of shoe boxes with names on them had been lined up neatly under the bed. Why?

She opened up one of the boxes and discovered it contained ashes. Maybe this was the only one that did, so she opened another. Same result: more ashes.

All of a sudden, her heart began to race, and she asked herself, *What the hell have I gotten myself into? I can't stay here.*

She told Rick about her discovery, and he said to ignore it. They would ask his mother about those in the morning.

"No way," she said. "We can't stay here."

Rick succeeded in calming her down, and she agreed to stay. Predictably, she did not sleep well.

When morning dawned, she got up and went into the kitchen, where Dorothy had already brewed the coffee.

Dorothy offered her a cup, but Teresa got right to the point. "Whose ashes are in those shoe boxes?"

"We don't believe in the afterlife or spending money on funerals," said Dorothy.

"What do you do with them?"

"In time, we just spread the ashes."

Teresa thought, *This is just too weird.*

She wouldn't be going anywhere without Rick, so she sat down for coffee and tried not to think about what she had seen. Tonight, they will sleep somewhere else.

After Rick had had breakfast, he suggested that he and Teresa take a ride over to the beach and that his mother could watch Little Ricky.

Teresa balked at this idea. After what she had seen, she would take the child with them wherever they went.

When Rick told his mother that he and Teresa were going to the beach, she offered to keep her grandchild so they could enjoy the day.

Teresa thanked her but declined, saying, "This is his first trip to the beach. We don't know when we'll get back, but thank you."

"Well, make sure you use sunscreen on him," said Dorothy.

"Oh, we will," replied Teresa.

On the way to the beach, Teresa told Rick about her conversation with his mother.

"I told you my family was weird," he said.

That night, the couple slept in another room, and this was their room for the remainder of their visit. Teresa found nothing weird in this one, but she didn't look too closely. She figured she would feel more comfortable not finding things. In just a couple more days, she and Rick would return home. And get back to normal.

When the time came to say good-bye to his family, Dorothy hugged them both. Crystal hugged Rick, but not Teresa. Instead, she turned to her and said, "You take care."

"You do the same."

Crystal watched Teresa from the time of their exchange until Teresa's car was no longer in view.

During the ride back to Virginia, Rick asked Teresa what she thought of Florida.

"It's a nice place to visit."

"Would you ever want to live there?" he asked.

"No. It wouldn't feel like home. I don't want to be that far away from my family."

"But you like the beach, don't you?"

"Not enough to move there."

"I was thinking we could sell our home and move to Florida," said Rick.

"No way. That's not happening."

Rick sulked. Teresa kept driving.

Once home, they unpacked and got ready to return to work the next day. Routinely, Teresa took Little Ricky to her aunt's home, which was just three miles away.

About two weeks following their return home from Florida, Teresa received a letter from a credit card company, which explained that the company would seek legal action if payment was not made promptly.

She was confused. She did not have an account with this company. She called the business and was told that an application for a credit card had been submitted identifying her as the person requesting the card. All her identifiers had been provided, and the application had been approved. Rick apparently requested that his name also be on the card so that he could use it. Two cards had been sent to their address, but she had never seen them. She learned that they had been approved for a credit line of $3,000 and that he had already used the maximum allowed and had not made any payments toward this debt.

She said she knew nothing about this but that she would promptly discuss the matter with Rick.

That night, she did just that.

Initially evasive, he finally admitted that he had taken the card out in their names, but for good reason. He told her he wanted to start his own handyman business and needed some things to get the business going. He reasoned that after the business was up and running, he could pay off this debt in the near future.

This was disconcerting to her. She worked hard, lived responsibly, and paid the bills promptly. He had done this without consulting with her, and his actions had a personal impact on her.

Adding this act of fiscal irresponsibility to the list of Rick's wrongdoings—which already included excessive drinking, habitual gambling, and the possibility of infidelity—she questioned whether marriage had really been her best option.

Though he worked regularly, he often told her he was low on money and could not help her out with some of the bills. She wondered why and later found out that he had gambled away much of his earnings. Occasionally, after a night of working at the restaurant, he would go to parties and drink so much that he passed out. One of his friends would call her to let her know of his location, and like the faithful wife she was, she would go get him and bring him home.

Of all of his transgressions, the one that concerned her most was the reports of his infidelity. Not only was that hurtful to her and destructive to their relationship, but it also posed health risks in the form of sexually transmitted diseases.

Still, she always found room in her heart to forgive him so their marriage continued. They still enjoyed going to Charles Town together, and they still enjoyed sex on those occasions when he was home.

Just a little over two years into their marriage, she became pregnant again. She felt elated. Being a mother came naturally to her. Like her mother, she was devoted.

Her only reservation was what she thought Rick's reaction would be.

But now that they had been married for a time, perhaps he would be much more receptive to the news of another pregnancy.

Soon after learning she was pregnant, she came home from work, fixed a nice dinner, and waited for him to come home. She reasoned that after consuming a good meal, he would be at his best to receive the news.

Right on time, she told him she had something to tell him after he had finished eating.

"What is it?" he asked.

She hesitated, smiled, and then said, "I'm pregnant."

A silence followed. She needed him to say something.

"What do you think?"

"Holy shit," he said. "I'm not ready for this."

"*You* aren't ready?"

"Hell no. I gotta think about this. I'll be back in a while." He left for the bar.

She cried. That night, she went to bed alone. She awoke when he heard him come through the back door and then he looked for leftovers in the kitchen to satisfy the midnight munchies.

When he later came into their bedroom, she pretended she was asleep.

The next morning, it was back to work. She decided not to broach the subject with him again for a few days. Maybe, she thought, he would come around.

But he didn't; instead, he gave her the worst advice she could imagine. "Why don't you get an abortion?" he asked.

"There is no damn way I would get an abortion," she shot back.

"It's gonna be hard for us to have the life we want," he said.

"The life we want? What is it you don't have?"

"I didn't expect we would have to raise a bunch of kids. I didn't want you to get pregnant the first time, and now you're pregnant again."

"Maybe my family will help me out if you're not interested in our children," she said.

"Oh, don't get them involved," he replied.

"Then you need to step up and take responsibility," she said.

That was the last of their discussion on the topic.

On May 17, 1995, she gave birth to fraternal twins—a girl and a boy. She named their daughter Ashley Nicole and their second son Allen Nathaniel.

They were now a family of five.

But she felt more like a single parent since Rick did his own thing for the most part. Still, he did have a few good moments.

One of Teresa's favorite photographs of Rick and their children was the one that depicted Rick and Ashley during Christmas of 1998. It captured a very happy little girl hugging her father's neck. He looked like a proud father in this photo.

Like any Christmas, Teresa took her share of pictures of the children at such a happy time. In one of those, the three children were posed in front of the Christmas tree. Ricky Junior and Ashley appeared extremely happy while Allen looked equally sad.

Teresa managed to smile whenever her picture was taken, but she had the habit of leaning her head to the left during those times. It was something she did without thinking about it.

Soon after this Christmas, rumors began to circulate again that Rick was involved with another woman. She vowed that if the rumors turned out to be true this time, then she would put him out and be done with him.

Word had it that the woman with whom Rick was involved lived a few miles away in the town of Orange. Maybe Teresa could find out where this woman lived and catch them in the act.

Tammy advised her to hire a private detective. Tammy said she knew someone who had hired one, and it had worked. Teresa considered the idea but was soon distracted when she received a telephone call from Aunt Doris, who said she was out of a few things, including diapers.

Teresa agreed to go home at lunch and collect the things needed and bring them to her. As she approached her home, she noticed that both of Rick's vehicles were in the driveway. Funny thing: he was supposed to be at work.

Instead, he was in their bed with another woman.

Teresa's previously pent-up fury was finally unleashed. As the adulterous woman jumped out the window, Teresa looked to the corner of the room and saw what they called the club—a steering wheel lock, which she now turned into a weapon. She soon struck Rick with it and continued to strike at him until she had herded him out the back door. Once he got through it, he immediately took off running and heard her yelling, "Don't ever come back!"

The scorned wife then used the club for its intended purpose—to lock the steering wheel on Rick's pickup truck. She also took his keys and hid them.

After she regained her wits, she collected the things she needed for the children and headed to Doris's house, where she told her aunt what had happened. Doris told her she should call the police, and also to collect a few clothes to stay with her for a few days until things settled down.

She called the police and was told there was nothing they could do unless she formally pressed charges. She decided not to press charges, and not to stay with her aunt.

She saw no reason why Rick's unfaithfulness should uproot her or her children. They would stay.

Over the next four months, the troubled couple spoke by telephone, and she allowed him to come to the house long enough to retrieve his belongings, including his vehicles. She understood that he had taken up residence with the same woman who had bolted naked from Teresa's home.

Maybe Rick came to his senses and recognized that in Teresa he had married a good woman and a devoted mother. Maybe that explained why he later called her and begged him to take her back. Once again, Teresa proved forgiving, but this time conditionally. She agreed to let him come home if he would seek help for his drinking and adulterous behavior. He agreed to the terms and moved back home.

This next arrangement lasted just a few months. Not only did Rick not seek counseling to address those issues, but he decided that he no longer wanted her or their children. He told her he no longer found her desirable, that she did not have what he needed in a woman. He gave her the green light to initiate divorce proceedings.

When he went to work the next day, she promptly put his clothes back in the yard and called him and told him to have someone come and get them soon, or she would burn them. She then called the police and told them about the domestic situation and how she expected Rick to react.

Rick got the message about his clothes and came by to retrieve them without incident. He then began living from pillar to post until he settled in once more with the same woman while Teresa began the legal process that would make her a single parent.

9

AFTER THE LEGAL BATTLES, AN EERIE SILENCE

SHE SOON CALLED an attorney to begin the legal proceedings, which included the terms of separation, custody,
visitation, and child support.

Though Teresa had found Rick in bed with another
woman and could have substantiated a charge of adultery,
the separation agreement they signed mentioned nothing
of this; instead, it used the popular term "irreconcilable dif-
ferences" to identify the reason for their separation

Teresa was awarded custody of the children, and Rick
was ordered to pay child support. The agreement allowed
him visitation with the children every Sunday, with the

provision that someone other than him provided transportation, and that he not use alcohol or any other drugs.

Rick knew he could not win the legal battle but he attempted to win the battle for the children's minds.

He began to play mind games with Teresa and the children. He was angry his wife had made him leave and was not willing to take him back. He turned his anger toward the children. There were times when he told them their mother must not really love them because she kicked their daddy out of the home. In time, he convinced the oldest that this was true, and Ricky became verbally aggressive toward his mother. At school, he acted out in anger and was referred to a counselor. During those counseling sessions, it was learned that the basis for Ricky's anger and acting out stemmed from his father's mistreatment of him. He told his counselor that his father had called him names such as "pussy" and "queer boy," and that he sometimes poked is finger in his chest and told him he would never amount to anything.

Worse still, during those visitations, he did the unthinkable: he had sex with his live-in partner in front of the children, who promptly reported what they saw and heard to their mother. On top of that, he failed to comply with the provision that required he pay child support.

Teresa soon filed a motion to amend visitation, and once the matter was heard in court, the presiding judge modified the order pertaining to visitation to read that Rick would visit with the children monthly under the supervision of a social worker and at the children's home. The judge also admonished Rick for not complying with the requirement that he pay child support.

Rick adhered to the change in visitation terms for about six months, but he did not pay child support, so when he asked Teresa for permission to take the children to Florida to visit his mother, she flatly refused.

Soon afterward, he was jailed for driving while intoxicated, which resulted in a conviction and a few days in jail. This put him farther behind on the path of compliance with the court's orders.

Some of the marital accounts he and Teresa had established were still in both of their names, including a Lowe's charge card, which he promptly maxed out and then paid nothing toward the debt. By agreement, he was supposed to pay this debt and one other.

His sister Crystal telephoned Teresa one day and demanded that she allow Rick to return to their home. Teresa, of course, refused; and Crystal told her she would regret that decision.

Rick eventually moved to Crystal's home in the Tidewater area of Virginia, and soon ran afoul of the law. He incurred charges of credit card theft and fraud and was convicted and served three months in jail.

When he was released, he told Teresa he was a changed man and was living in Virginia Beach, where he had secured both gainful employment and his own residence. He asked her if he could bring the kids there so they could enjoy the beach. She refused.

Crystal soon intervened again and, with a softer delivery, asked Teresa if the children could visit her and her family at her residence in Gloucester. Teresa's heart had softened some, and she allowed it. For the next six months, Rick, whose driver's license had been suspended, showed up monthly to pick up the children and take them to Gloucester to visit with him and his family.

Teresa later had second thoughts about the wisdom of these arrangements, so she ended those trips. She told Rick he could only visit with the children locally.

Rick continued to have problems with the law, and he incurred more charges and convictions and served another period of incarceration. All the while, he was racking up a huge debt of unpaid child support, leaving Teresa to fend for the children by herself.

She was struggling to support herself and the three children. While she had been fiscally responsible and had always worked regularly, the job at the factory was not a high-paying one; and as the kids grew older and their needs changed, she could have used financial assistance.

With Rick dilatory in his support, she turned to the Department of Social Services for assistance, but did not qualify.

Crystal devised a scheme to take control away from Teresa. Once Rick had served his most recent period of incarceration, she told him she would attempt to gain custody of the children. Given Rick's history of adulterous and irresponsible behavior, coupled with Teresa's motherly devotion, this was a preposterous suggestion. Nevertheless, Crystal filed a petition for a change of custody. The court immediately appointed a guardian *ad litum* to represent the children; and about five months later, the case was finally heard.

The judge did not award custody to Crystal but modified visitation to allow Rick to visit with the children with no other family members present. Because Rick had reneged on his obligation to pay any child support, the judge told Teresa she could consider filing a petition for child support through the Division of Child Support Enforcement, and the total amount of child support would be determined retroactively with the start date being the date of the couple's separation. Rick was livid. He soon learned he owed approximately $14,000 in child support.

What to do about it? Disappear. The only time he was heard from was over Christmas, when he would call Teresa and ask to speak to the children. On those rare occasions, he told her he would honor his child support obligation, but he never did. In time, she petitioned the court to have him brought back for failure to pay support.

The court granted her petition and set a date for the hearing. The clerk sent notice by mail to Rick about the time and date of the hearing but he did not appear. The court then issued a summons for his appearance, which went unserved. Law enforcement officials could not locate him.

Meanwhile, Crystal succeeded in getting her mother to call Teresa and seek permission to see the children at their home. Teresa consented; she had no reason that she knew of to deny Dorothy the opportunity to see her grandchildren. Dorothy had done nothing wrong, and Teresa had always felt sympathy for her.

She told Dorothy she could visit the children at her home, so Dorothy made arrangements to come to Virginia.

On the day that Dorothy was scheduled to visit, Crystal made a surprise and unwelcome visit as well. A confrontation between Crystal and Teresa ensued, and Teresa ordered them to leave while she called the police. An officer soon showed up and quickly assessed the situation. He told Dorothy and Crystal that they had to leave, which they did.

Teresa assumed that Rick's family would make its next move. Instead, an eerie silence set in, and she did not hear from Rick or any of his family for almost three years. Nevertheless, she looked over her shoulder every day, expecting an unwanted visit.

In time, it happened.

On a Wednesday evening, after she had returned home, served dinner, and helped the children with their homework, she heard a knock on the side door.

She went to the door, and there was Rick.

"I want to come back home," he said.

"You can't," she replied. "It's over. It's been over."

"I'll even stay in the outbuildings if you let me come back," he pleaded.

"No, Rick. I loved you, but I don't love you anymore. The best thing that came out of our relationship is our children, and I would die for them."

Reluctantly, he nodded and then left.

She soon learned that he had returned to the local area and was living with an older man who was an alcoholic. He had also returned to work at Clyde's Family Restaurant. He even began paying child support and occasionally sent flowers to her.

No way would she ever reunite with him, but she loved her children and wanted them to have a relationship with their father. She agreed to let him see them every other weekend.

Soon, he reverted to his old ways. He took out another credit card in her name and ran up the charges. She pressed charges, and he was later convicted of credit card fraud in 2005. He served six months in jail, and when he was released, he returned to Virginia Beach.

It occurred to her that he had been in and out of jail over a period of five years, from 2000 to 2005. This reminder convinced her that she had made the right decision to divorce him. The divorce decree was entered on October 9, 2003. He had not proven stable. It was best this way for her and the children.

The Thanksgiving and Christmas holidays were approaching, and she prepared to make this holiday season a happy one.

10

EVIL CLAIMS ITS
FIRST VICTIM

BACK DURING THE summer of this year, 2005, Teresa had a premonition. She believed that harm would one day come to her. She knew it was inevitable.

To prepare for it, she went to Jenny's home and told her how she felt. Twice during their conversation, she pressed Jenny to promise her that if anything happened to her, Jenny would make sure the children stayed safe. Jenny quickly promised to do just that. Teresa was emphatic: "The kids cannot go live with those people."

Jenny was a loyal sister and confidant to Teresa. Though Teresa was thirteen years older, the two of them were especially close. Jenny had lived with her for four years, beginning when Jenny was twelve years old.

But Jenny was not the only person close to Teresa. All their siblings were close to one another, and they had always stuck together. This time would be no exception.

Two days before Thanksgiving Day, Teresa's telephone rang. She answered it, and Rick was on the other end. He told her he had just been released from jail, and this time he truly had changed. He wanted to come see the children. In the background, Ashley could tell that her parents were talking and she was excited at the prospect of seeing her father.

Thanksgiving was out of the question because Teresa and the children already had plans.

"What about Christmas?" he asked.

"I want to see him," Ashley blurted out.

Teresa thought about it, agreed, and then set the terms: Rick could have the children over Christmas, with the agreement he would pick them up on December 23 and bring them back home on December 26. Since Rick's driver's license was still suspended, he would have Crystal bring him.

The dates were set. Ashley was the most excited of the three children. Ricky and Allen were both ambivalent.

Like every holiday season, the time between Thanksgiving and Christmas was an accelerated blur. Before they knew it,

Christmas was upon them, and the children would go with their father.

On the twenty-third, Rick showed up with Crystal. He went to the door while Crystal waited in the car. Ashley greeted her father with a huge hug, and her brothers shook his hand.

Teresa hugged and kissed all the children and told them to have a great Christmas. If they needed her, all they had to do was call.

"Don't forget to have them back on the twenty-sixth," she reminded Rick.

"I will," he said.

Rick and the children got in the car. The children waved good-bye to their mother. Rick and Crystal did not look back.

The children were on their way to Gloucester, and perhaps to the unknown.

On Christmas Day, Teresa opted to stay at home. Traditionally, she spent time with family, but she felt too worried and didn't want to bring anyone else down. Christmas was supposed to be joyful.

Her mother called her to wish her a Merry Christmas and then turned the phone over to other family members who did the same. Jenny told her they could talk again tomorrow after the children had returned.

Home alone, Teresa went to bed early in anticipation of the children coming home the next day.

On December 26, she awoke early, made coffee, read the newspaper, and turned on the news. That distracted her for awhile; but for most of the rest of the day, she found herself gazing out the window, expecting to see her children pull up into the driveway.

Minutes turned to hours, and by 7:00 p.m., there was no word from Rick or the children.

Finally, she called Rick's cell phone, but her call went to voice mail. She left a message requesting that he call her to let her know what was going on.

Feeling some dread, she then called the family residence in Gloucester. She let the phone ring approximately ten times, but no one answered. Maybe, she thought, Rick, Crystal, and the children were en route to her house. They would need to be careful; it was beginning to sleet. The roads could become treacherous.

She went through the television stations and found a popular movie to watch. That helped some, but when it was over, there had still been no sign of the children.

She needed to talk to someone. She turned to the ever-reliable Jenny.

"I'm going crazy. Rick has not brought the children home."

"That bastard," said Jenny. "Has he even called you?"

"No, and I tried to call their home and got no answer."

"Maybe they're on their way," replied Jenny. "He never was very responsible, but I don't think he would just not show up knowing how you are about the children. He's been in court a few times and should know by now."

"I made a huge mistake," said an emotional Teresa. "I should have never let him take those kids. That sister of his is evil."

"You hang in there," said Jenny. "I'm on my way to see you."

Jenny cried as she apprised her husband, Dwayne, of the situation. He said, "She's your sister. You do what you gotta do. Just be careful."

Before Jenny could get out the door, the phone rang.

It was Teresa.

"Don't come over. The roads are getting bad. It's been sleeting, and you could wreck. I'll be okay. I'll call you whenever I hear from them. I have to go to work in the morning and don't want to go unless the kids are here."

"Anything you need us to do we'll do for you," said Jenny. "You should call the police. You have full custody of those kids. He has no right to keep them from you. He gave you his word he would bring them back today, and he hasn't. The police can help you."

"I might," replied Teresa. "But you don't know what kind of people I'm dealing with. Anyway, I'll see you soon."

Teresa went to bed that night in an empty house.

The following day, it was back to work for her and for Jenny.

At 8:30 a.m., Jenny was on the job when a coworker informed her she had a telephone call.

Jenny went to the administrative office and took the phone.

"Ms. Dodson?"

"Yes, this is her."

"Ms. Dodson, this is Trooper Anderson with the Virginia State Police."

———✳———

Jenny looked at Teresa's swollen and darkened face. She noted the expression of horror, which Jenny later said "told a million stories."

Even though the trooper told Jenny he would soon be over, Jenny called 911 anyway. While she was on the phone with the dispatcher, Trooper Anderson appeared. Jenny told the dispatcher, "Never mind. The police are already here."

Jenny went around to the back of the house to see if any of the windows had been broken, but they had not.

One of the neighbors, a Mr. Henshaw, saw the trooper's car in the driveway and came over to see what was going on.

Trooper Anderson asked Mr. Henshaw if he had seen or heard anything suspicious last night.

"I'll tell you the truth. I heard a scream last night, like that of a young child."

"Did you see anybody?"

"No, sir, I didn't."

Trooper Anderson even questioned Jenny and wanted to know where she had been the night before.

Her indignation was tempting, but Jenny simply answered his questions. She must keep her wits. She was the strongest link to Teresa. In this moment, Jenny proved to be a quick thinker.

She checked Teresa's cell phone for Rick's telephone numbers. She jotted down his cell number and then dialed it using Teresa's home phone, knowing that this number would show up on Rick's phone if he answered it.

After just two rings, Rick answered with a question.

"Jenny, what's wrong? Is anybody at the house?"

How did Rick know Jenny was on the other end of the call? She had yet to say anything. She skipped the formalities and any unnecessary exchange of pleasantries and demanded, "Bring those children home immediately. I mean it."

He agreed to bring them in the morning. End of conversation.

Soon Jenny's siblings arrived. Jenny, with some help from her brothers, succeeded in changing the locks on the doors and then went through the house collecting important paperwork.

In the morning, Jenny was appalled to witness her nephew, Ricky Junior, just twelve years of age, driving the vehicle that contained a number of passengers—Rick, his mother, a woman whose hair completely covered her face, and the twins. They were all packed in a mid-sized sedan. All three of the adults were obviously intoxicated.

Rick, Jr., with Allen under his wing, and Ashley right behind them, rushed from the car to the door where Jenny was prepared to meet them with a warm embrace. Jenny could see that all three of the children were crying. The twins raced past her and began looking for their mother while Rick, Jr. groaned and then blurted out, "It's all my fault. If I hadn't left her alone she would be here."

He quickly sat down in deep despair.

The twins went to their mother's bedroom where Ashley threw herself on the bed, sank her face into a pillow, and continued to cry.

Allen soon returned to see Jenny and was frantic. He kept asking, Where is she? Where is she? I want to see her. I really want to see her now," over and over it seemed to Jenny. She reached out to hug him hoping to console him but he twisted away. He could not be consoled.

Before his father could stumble his way inside the home, Allen blurted out:

"I don't believe what my dad says. He lies ALL the time."

Jenny took a quick peak outside to check the status of the adults whose intoxication made them slow with their approach to the house.

"What do you mean you don't believe what your dad says?"

"He told us her heart gave out on her."

When did he tell you that?

"When we were at Walmat."

"You mean in Gloucester?"

"Yes."

"When did this happen?

"A couple of days after Christmas. He took us for some Christmas presents. I wanted to get a present for momma and he said you don't need to. Her heart stopped on her."

With Ashley on her mother's bed crying and Allen struggling to come to grips, older brother Rick, Jr. sat motionless in a chair with his head down.

Jenny looked over at him hoping to make eye contact and offer words of comfort. Rick, Jr. never looked up but she could see the tears streaming down both cheeks.

The next instant, Rick Sr. and his entourage came in.

Once inside, Jenny took charge and said she had some questions for Rick, who was in no mood to be interrogated.

"He immediately blurted out, "It's none of your fucking business. This house is mine. Y'all get the hell out of it."

As soon as she heard her father's voice, Ashley bolted from the bedroom and stood next to her father. Ashley loved her mother but she also adored her father. With her mother dead, her father was now her only parent.

She had heard the exchange between Jenny and her father and she immediately took his side.

Jenny did not wilt. Unbeknownst to Rick, she had Teresa's gun concealed on her person.

"You'll have to take my life to get it," she said. "You don't intimidate me. If you would like to see what you gave to my sister, I'm on to you. You and whatever you call it can all get out of this house."

Ashley spoke up and said, "He's all I've got left."

Just as Ashley blurted out her support for her father, her older brother finally looked up and made eye contact. He did so with his father and he had something important to tell him.

"I hope you're happy now. You stole the last minutes I could have had with her and I will hate you the rest of my life."

His father's cavalier attitude continued as he waged his power struggle with Jenny.

Never mind what his son had just said to him.

Rick then was brazen enough to ask Jenny if Teresa had been seeing the same doctor. "Where is she?" he asked. "I want to see her body. You might as well tell me. I have ways of finding out where she's at."

Because Ashley desperately did not want her father to leave, a strange sort of sleepover took place. Rick, the person whom Jenny strongly suspected of killing Teresa, and his mother and an unknown woman all stayed under the same roof with the children and Jenny and her siblings.

Jenny's husband brought coffee to her and her siblings to help them stay awake through the night as they stayed on guard for what Rick might do.

That night, Rick snuck out of Teresa's bedroom window after Ashley had fallen asleep. Jenny soon learned that he had taken some of the children's Christmas gifts that their mother had purchased for them back to the store to be exchanged for money.

When he returned, he could not get in. The locks had been changed, and Jenny left him standing outside. Meanwhile, Ashley started going through her mother's closet and found the Christmas gifts intended for them. These were still wrapped. Rick had taken the gifts that had not been wrapped.

Eventually, Jenny let Rick back in the house. He watched the children unwrap the remaining gifts, which turned out to be electronic devices. Rick insisted on taking them, but first he asked for the receipts.

"What the hell are you thinking?" Jenny asked him.

"It won't matter," he said. "She's dead."

"How do you know she's dead?" asked Jenny.

"You said so."

"No. I didn't say a word."

Jenny immediately went off on Rick for stealing the gifts while one of her brothers jerked Rick up by his collar. It was then that they noticed Rick had a terrible gash on his left leg. Their oldest sister, Annette, told him he should have the wound checked out by a doctor. Rick demanded answers about Teresa. Since Jenny and her siblings would not give them to him, he left and went to Teresa's doctor's office, where he demanded that the doctor tell him the whereabouts of Teresa's body. The doctor refused, so Rick went to the funeral home and demanded to see the body. He was told the body was not there. He told them that when it arrived, he wanted it immediately cremated. He was told to take this matter up with the family. He left, enraged.

Jenny had called the funeral home to warn them that Rick would likely show up and what he might do. She also made arrangements for family night.

What Rick did not know, and what Jenny would never tell him, was that Teresa's body had been moved to Northern

Virginia at her request. Rick was convinced that the body was in Richmond, and he had Crystal call there to confirm.

Without confirmation, Rick and Crystal could only speculate as to its location.

Rick went back to the house and demanded to know what was going on. He told them to all get out. Jenny then called the police. Before the police arrived, Crystal showed up in a van with a dog she turned loose.

Rick told Jenny, "If I have to leave this property, the kids are leaving with me, and they won't get to see her funeral."

Crystal soon began helping herself to some of Teresa's belongings, but when the officer arrived, he made her return the property. Eventually, Rick and his sister left and were not seen again until family night.

On that night, Rick showed up in the company of his brother-in-law, Buddy, who was married to Crystal, and with three other men, who all wore black trench coats.

Teresa lay in the casket, and Jenny stayed close to her.

Jenny had called the police and told them she expected trouble at family night. An off-duty police officer stood behind the casket and had already called for backup when Rick approached Jenny, leaned over the casket, and said to her, "Do you like the way she looks? You better take this seriously and get out of my way. Shut your fat mouth, or I promise you that you will look like her tomorrow."

Jenny thrust her leg into the coffin and asked, "Is that a threat or a promise?"

People began to scatter as Rick pointed a gun at her.

"Go ahead," said Jenny. "Get it over with."

The officer quickly intervened and told Rick to hand over the gun, which he did without incident.

One of Jenny's nieces, who had been watching carefully, struck Rick and knocked him out. While he was on the floor, she said, "Be a good father, you son of a bitch."

The officer directed Rick's friends to the back of the office, and help soon arrived. They were escorted out and told not to come back.

Jenny learned that they were staying in a neighboring county.

The funeral was held the next day. Jenny, with the assistance of her brother Billy Lee brought the children. Older brother Doug stayed at Teresa's home just in case Rick showed up and caused any trouble. Doug would not hesitate to go from a verbal altercation to a physical one.

At the funeral, Jenny wept. But she also looked over her shoulder constantly, thinking she would see Rick or some of his family.

He and his family did not attend, but later that day, Crystal called Jenny and delivered this threat: "You got yours coming."

Jenny shrugged it off and immediately contacted the court and requested an emergency hearing to determine custody—at least temporary—of the children.

The judge granted custody to Jenny, and they remained in her care with the assistance of her family. They devised a plan that called for the children to stay at two different places at different times, which would help keep them safe.

This arrangement had been in place for about three months when Crystal notified Jenny that Rick had decided he wanted custody of the children.

The fight was on.

11

THE MOLE FINDS ITS WAY

JENNY HAD ALREADY proven a thoughtful and resourceful person during the crisis she and her family had faced. Not only had she immediately gone to work on security matters following Teresa's death, but she also had begun her own brand of investigation into the background of the person she was certain was responsible for her sister's death. That person, of course, was Rick.

First, she and her family had never liked him, and she had expressed to Teresa the bad vibe he gave her from the beginning.

Second, the conversation she had with him on the day she found Teresa's dead body reinforced her belief that he was guilty.

Third, his conduct following Teresa's death was additional evidence to her conclusion, notably that he had demanded that her body be cremated, which she presumed meant would avoid an autopsy report that would reveal the cause of death.

Then, too, she remembered her conversation with Teresa following the Christmas in 1992, when she expressed her concern that she was involved with a man about whose background she knew so little. At that time, Teresa had not even met Rick's family. To Jenny, that was a red flag that Teresa had overlooked.

Curious herself as to the circumstances that brought Rick to Virginia, Jenny soon learned what she wished Teresa had known early on.

Her discoveries might have been the envy of every private investigator.

At the time Rick came to Virginia, he was running from charges in Florida, which included second degree murder. With the aid of his sister Crystal, who Jenny learned had run a prostitution ring earlier in her life, Rick fled north in the trunk of Crystal's car, which traveled across the Georgia, South Carolina, and North Carolina state lines before stopping in Greensboro.

There, Crystal and Rick took up residence, and Rick found work at a local restaurant by night and did tree work during the day.

About a month into their stay, Crystal met the man she would eventually marry, Buddy Stringfield—a hard-drinking and rough-looking tractor trailer driver who had family ties in the Tidewater area of Virginia.

When Crystal and Buddy married, they soon relocated to Tidewater, and Rick went with them. Unable to find the type of employment he wanted, Rick learned that the factory in Culpeper was hiring, so he applied for the job and was hired. He then relocated to the local area and rented an apartment in Orange, where the rent was cheaper than that in Culpeper. Plus, he landed the second job at Clyde's.

In addition to finding out what she could about Rick and his background, Jenny took all the precautions she could think of to protect the children, to make sure they attended school, and that they were provided for. This included her filing a petition for their custody. Teresa had included a provision in her last will and testament that expressed her wish that should something happen to her, the children should not be required to live with Rick's family. She viewed them as unsavory characters.

Crystal stepped in and said that Rick wanted custody.

Before the case could be settled in court, Crystal made a bold move: she showed up at the elementary school the twins attended and picked them up. Rick Junior attended middle school at the time and Jenny was able to intervene before Crystal attempted to pick him up. She also called the police, and they succeeded in returning the children to Jenny.

Jenny recalled that they appeared in court a total of four times with custody on the line. During three of those hearings, the court ruled in her favor. At the fourth hearing, the judge decided to meet with each of the three children and asked each where they wanted to live. Ashley was adamant that she wanted to live with her father; Rick Junior told the judge he would hang himself before he lived with his father, whom he described as "a deadbeat sperm donor"; and Allen wanted to stay with Jenny.

Later, Rick Junior requested that he be allowed to live with Jenny's brother and his wife, Michael and Lynn. He was afraid that his father would hurt Jenny if he continued to stay with her. Jenny agreed that Rick Junior could stay with them, but that she wanted visitation with him on the weekends.

In Teresa's last will and testament, there was a provision indicating that she nominated her brother Michael and her sister-in-law Lynn as guardians and caretakers of the children, and that visitation should continue with the father, but to be coordinated by Michael and Lynn.

Amid the legal battles and conflicts, an interesting twist to the story developed when Crystal forged an alliance of sorts with Lynn, which was aided by the fact that Ricky Junior and Lynn's oldest son had become best friends.

Crystal enticed the children to come live with her by giving gifts to them and taking them on trips.

It worked on Ricky Junior. He realized that the city had much more to offer, and he began making excuses not to see Jenny, who insisted that the three children visit with her as one. Ricky Junior was now Rick Junior, and he resisted and accused Jenny of being a control freak.

At the next hearing, Lynn testified in court that the children would be better off with their father, who she said deserved a second chance. The judge felt compelled to send Rick Junior to live with his father, which he did. Ashley was eager to go, but Allen cried at the prospect. He did not want to leave his home, but he didn't want to be separated from his brother and his sister either.

When Jenny testified, the opposing attorney asked her if her pursuit of continued custody was about the money and nothing else. Jenny testified that she had never received any money. She was concerned only for the welfare of her children. At that time, Rick owed over $15,000 in arrears for child support, and Jenny insisted that he pay the money and that it go into a trust.

The judge gave Jenny discretion when it came to handling the financial component. After the hearing, the children packed their bags and, with tears in their eyes, left for their new home.

Crystal and Buddy promptly cut off communications with Jenny and her family, except for Michael and Lynn. They were the only two allowed to talk to the children or to visit with them.

Based on the provision in Teresa's last will and testament, Lynn had some legal latitude with the children, but she later signed over her legal rights to Crystal, without Jenny or anyone else in their family knowing.

During the spring of 2007, the children wanted to see their mother's side of the family and invited them to attend their birthday party at their home in Gloucester. Jenny and her family gladly accepted the invitation.

12

SHADES OF DARKNESS

CONSIDERING ALL THAT Jenny knew about Rick and his family, it naturally caused her some anxiety to think she would now be on his and his family's turf.

Thankfully, she did not make the trip alone. All her family, including her mother, made the trip to Gloucester. In the presence of her brothers, Jenny could always feel safe.

But as soon as they arrived, her suspicions were confirmed.

"That was truly when we learned what kind of characters they were," Jenny later recalled. "Their house was something you would see in a drug dealer's world. They had a six-car garage, an in-ground pool that was marble granite and surrounded by palm trees. In the garages, they had Shelby Mustangs and limited-edition Harley-Davidsons. There were surveillance cameras in every room, even the bathrooms. They had four commercial-size greenhouses located on the property and about twenty men dressed in leather and wearing dark sunglasses who walked around the pool. They communicated with each other using their cell phones."

Jenny had a hard time wrapping her head around the idea that people who purportedly operated a tree company could live so lavishly.

Crystal took Jenny on a tour of the house. The bedrooms were located on the third floor. In between the master bedroom and its bathroom was a huge walk-in closet with mirrored doors that disguised a studio.

Jenny couldn't help but ask Crystal about the purpose of having all those cameras.

"We have so many expensive things," said Crystal. "We wouldn't want anyone to steal them."

Later, Jenny and her mother, Martha, had the opportunity to talk to Rick's mother, Dorothy, alone.

"Where is Rick?" Martha asked Dorothy.

Dorothy cried and then said, "You don't know?

"Know what?'

"He's dead."

"What happened?" asked Jenny.

Dorothy looked around before she answered.

"My baby was murdered. And to think that my own blood could do such a thing. I feel like I'm trapped in a web of black widow spiders. All he wanted was to have his three babies back. He owed his sister some money, and he refused to pay it back, so she had him killed." Jenny then learned that Crystal had collected the proceeds from Rick's insurance policy, and then Dorothy led Jenny and Martha into the dining room area and showed them the box of ashes.

Jenny and Martha felt that their lives were in danger, and so they approached the other family members and told them it was best that they all leave. When everyone was together, Jenny told the children they had to leave. When Jenny walked around the corner of the house, she saw Crystal and Lynn signing papers. When they realized that Jenny was standing there, they pretended they were looking at pictures. Jenny acted like nothing was wrong but told them she had to leave.

As soon as Jenny and her family had left the property, they immediately went to the local police department, where they were promptly told to leave the county.

This family may have been strong, but not strong enough to take on law enforcement. They left, and about forty minutes later, Crystal called Jenny's cell phone and told her to never come back.

"Your actions will catch up with you one day," Jenny told Crystal. "You will get your karma."

Jenny and her family would have to wait for that.

They did not hear from the children again until Christmas of that year. The children stayed with Michael and Lynn over Christmas break, and Lynn called her mother-in-law and told her she was going to bring the children to see her. Martha was in a nursing home but called Jenny to let her know that Lynn was on her way.

Jenny left for the nursing home in time to find Lynn and the children there.

During the entire visit, Jenny noticed that Lynn hovered around the children and listened closely to what they told their grandmother.

This was no time for Jenny to pull any punches. When she was out of hearing range of the children, she turned to Lynn and said, "You're a witch on a broom. You're just in this for the kids' social security and their insurance money. Your day will come, and I hope I'm around to see it."

Lynn replied, "You won't get to see the children again if you keep acting this way."

"The kids are just hollow shells," said Jenny. "They are so brainwashed now that it won't make any difference if I see them again. Their lives were destroyed the day they left here. I'm going to report you and Crystal for fraud and for misusing their social security money."

After the Christmas break, the children returned to Gloucester. Jenny didn't make promises she didn't intend to keep, so she soon sought legal action.

She knew of Teresa's fiscal responsibility. Teresa had paid off all her debts two years prior to her death. In her last will and testament, she provided that her assets would divided equally among the three children, but that those monies would not be available to them until they reached the age of twenty-one.

When Teresa's estate and its contents were sold, Jenny took the money and put it into three separate accounts for the children. Teresa had been able to save a sum of money, plus she had taken out a life insurance policy and had a 401K through her employer.

She suspected Lynn and Crystal had taken money that belonged to the children, so she contacted the Department of Social Services to report the improprieties. The department looked into the matter, but decided not to take any action.

Jenny decided to call Lynn and question her about the insurance money that was due the kids following the death of their father.

Lynn could not account for the money, so Jenny went to the circuit court to file the papers.

Court records indicated there was an estate hearing in which it was determined that Jenny and her oldest sisters had been named as executors of Teresa's estate, whose assets included her house, which was assessed as having a value of about $45,000. The assets were to be passed on to the children, but to be held in trust until such time when they turned twenty-one. Nothing else was on file.

After Rick's death, Jenny and her family experienced a relative calm, but they had few opportunities to see the children.

When Jenny considered the facts, she reminded herself that Teresa had died two days after Christmas in 2005 and Rick died about a year and a half later. That was enough grief for any family to have to endure.

Unfortunately, that was not the end of it. What happened next was nothing short of horrifying.

13

TRAGIC ACCIDENT OR GRISLY MURDER?

Two years following the death of their father, the three children attempted to live happy and normal lives. The twins did remarkably well. They excelled in school and had many friends. The pictures taken of them show them as happy, well-cared-for young adults.

Allen wore glasses, and he kept his hair short. When he posed for the camera, he often had his hands in his pockets.

In her pictures, Ashley always looked happy and healthy. She could often be playful. Her smile always looked genuine.

Rick Junior stood straight up and smiled for the camera, but his smile looked partial rather than full. He too wore his hair short, and he sported a short beard.

The three of them continued to live with their paternal aunt Crystal and her husband, Buddy, who owned a tree and lawn care company after previously working as a tractor trailer driver.

What the pictures did not depict was that Rick Junior was afflicted by his abuse of alcohol and other drugs.

Then too, how could Jenny or any of her family truly know how the children were doing?

In September of 2009, Jenny and some of her family had occasion to see the children. At that time, Crystal and Buddy brought the children to the nursing home where the children's maternal grandmother was a resident. As it happened, Jenny and some of her siblings were there as well.

During the visit, there came a time when Allen told everyone he needed to retrieve something from their vehicle.

Alertly, Jenny decided to follow him.

"Are you okay?" she asked him.

Allen hesitated, looked around to see if anyone was within hearing distance, and then said, "I hate life. I want to come back home. I want my mother back and the way things used to be. I feel like a caged animal that's not getting any air."

"What's going on?" Jenny asked.

"If you knew, it would be dangerous for your family. I'm living with some evil people. They're like rats, and they'll eat anything. I know I'm not going to live to be an old man, but at least if I die, no one can hurt me again."

Jenny replied, "I'm going to get you out of this situation if I have to die."

But Allen wouldn't budge. "They will see us all dead before they will let you get custody of us. Promise me you won't tell my Aunt Crystal anything I told you. My brother and sister are brainwashed. They tell me it's all in my imagination and that I need to just let Mom rest."

Jenny then said, "If you decide to run away, don't tell anyone. Call me and I'll come get you."

Allen felt so hopeless he simply shrugged his shoulders, as if he believed his fate had already been sealed.

He then said, "However it turns out, I'll be with my mom. I miss her so much. My wish is to be with her and to be at home."

Crystal and Buddy took the children back to Gloucester with the holidays just around the corner.

Jenny prayed for the children daily and pondered what, if any, options she had at this point. Before she could take any sort of action, disaster struck four days before Thanksgiving.

On the Sunday before Thursday's Thanksgiving Day, Allen, who was fourteen years old at the time, was operating his uncle's wood chipper when suddenly the shovel he was using got caught in the blades and then sucked him into the chipper, where he died instantly and violently.

After his family called 911, not only did the police show up, but so did the media.

The obvious questions immediately surfaced. Why would a fourteen-year-old be allowed to operate such equipment? When the shovel got caught in the blades, could he have simply let go of the shovel and saved himself? Where were his legal guardians at the time?

In his obituary, Allen was described as a good student who was very popular: he loved sports, he loved cars, and he loved his Aunt Crystal.

This may all be true. But people don't write their own obituaries, and Allen is no longer around to tell authorities what was going on in the home.

The day following this tragic event, Jenny and her family received a telephone call from Crystal, who told them what had happened.

Jenny left the next morning for Gloucester. When she showed up, Crystal and Buddy seemed caught off guard by her presence. Jenny recalled just how crowded the home was. Allen had been so popular that the home was overflowing with friends from school and genuinely concerned members of the community who had heard the news. A local television station crew had set up at the end of the driveway and told the viewers the story.

Jenny remembers that at the funeral, the scene could have been used in a movie. There were too many Harley-

Davidsons to count, whose riders were men with sinister faces.

Jenny suspected foul play, especially when she learned that the wood chipper had been modified to allow an operator to turn it on and off with just a screwdriver.

Once more, Jenny felt helpless to do anything. She had known long before that Teresa would be hurt, and she always suspected that the children would be hurt in time.

Two of her worst nightmares had come true.

EPILOGUE

As would be expected, Buddy, who owned the wood chipper that took the life of Allen Koenig, was soon the subject of investigations by both the Commonwealth of Virginia and by the Occupational Safety and Health Administration (OSHA), which is a federal organization and part of the Department of Labor.

In the latter's investigation, OSHA noted that Virginia's child labor laws prohibit anyone under the age of eighteen from operating power woodworking machines, and that the wood chipper fell into this category. OSHA eventually leveled a hefty fine against Buddy since he was the owner of the machinery.

He was also charged with one felony—child cruelty—and several misdemeanors involving equipment violations.

As for the felony, an order of Nolle Prosequi was entered in the circuit court. In the common vernacular, this Latin term is often reflected as "Nolle Prossed," which indicates that the Attorney for the Commonwealth, for whatever reason(s), decided not to prosecute the case, which ended the matter at that time. It remains subject to future prosecution at the discretion of the Commonwealth should any additional evidence arise that would justify reopening the case.

Jenny learned that Buddy and the judge who presided over this case are distant cousins.

Buddy was convicted of one of the misdemeanors in the lower court of the county in which he resides.

Jenny shudders when she thinks about the grisly death little Allen endured. She is certain he grieved over the loss of his mother up to the very time he died.

Rick Junior, twenty-two, is a survivor. He has benefited from intense counseling and therapy. He has not only survived the tragic loss of his parents and a sibling, but he has also battled his addiction to alcohol and other drugs. He currently lives apart from his aunt and uncle and appears to have moved on with his life. To this day, he still blames himself for his mother's death. As the oldest sibling, he believes it was his responsibility to protect her, and he failed.

Ashley, twenty, also benefited from counseling and appears to have overcome much of the adversity. She is currently in her third year in college, where she lives on campus.

Both of them have little contact these days with their mother's family. Jenny decided that it is best to give them space and time.

The one thing she can always do for them is pray for them. This she does daily.

AFTERWORD

DURING THE COURSE of completing the manuscript for my first book, *Criminal Minds in Real Time,* my wife introduced me to a lady, to whom this book is dedicated and to whom I refer to as "G," who told us the tragic story of how her sister and one of her sister's three children had lost their lives.

As she has from the beginning, "G" remains convinced that her family members were murdered. Several years post death, the cases have not been solved, and there may be reason to believe that a segment of law enforcement is not genuinely interested in solving the cases. Perhaps there are those among them who were themselves complicit in the deaths. Perhaps time, which tends to reveal the truth about most things, will one day provide the answers.

Not only did I dedicate this book to her, but I also asked "G" for her suggestion when it came to the book's title. Considering all that has happened, and what has not happened, the book's title makes perfect sense.

Teresa's autopsy report indicated that there was no sign of injury. The cause of death is listed as "mitral valve prolapse," which occurs when the valve between the heart's left upper chamber and left lower chamber do not close properly. In layman's terms, one would conclude that Teresa died as a result of a defective heart.

The Department of Forensic Science completed its investigation and, in its Certificate of Analysis, indicated that Teresa had in her system at the time of her death 0.10% ethanol and the presence of Ibuprofen. That was it.

Did Teresa's heart give out because of the stress she was under? Of course, that is possible given the defect but the timing arouses dark suspicions, especially given Rick's demeanor on the telephone with Jenny when he assumed Jenny was on the other end. He began with asking her the question, "What's wrong?" Of course he knew that at least one thing was wrong: he had not brought the children back on the agreed date. How did he know that Jenny was on the other end of the phone? Was he watching from a distance or had he been there the night before and knew that Jenny would be along in the morning?

Obviously, the results of the autopsy left law enforcement no choice: they had no grounds to charge Rick or anyone else.

As for Rick, his death remains a complete mystery to "G" and her family. They simply don't know how he died.

His obituary said he died at the age of 41, had worked for a tree and lawn care company, and that he loved his family who meant everything to him.

Considering all that happened to this family, it is understandable that "G" and her family feel the system let them down which makes it difficult to come to terms with death. Too many questions remain unanswered such as, why did Teresa, a devoted mother and hard worker who lived so responsibly, have to die several years before her 50th birthday? Why did Allen, who was so well liked by his peers and had done so well in both academics and athletics, have to die so tragically as a young teenager? Was the love of money really at the root of all the apparent evil? Are the material things in life really more important to some people than life itself? These are the questions the survivors ponder. The answers may not come in this lifetime.

As for "G" she was quite receptive to this story being told and admitted she would like to see the people responsible for the deaths of her sister and nephew brought to justice; however, she also believes that maybe it's best that the story end here. With her faith in God, she knows that nothing, short of Christ's return and the resurrection of the dead, can bring back her sister and her nephew.

"G" knew her sister as well as anyone. For a number of years "G" felt "Teresa" remained restless in the grave. In more recent times, she feels "Teresa" has finally found rest. Perhaps the grave's silence is solace enough until God's judgment is meted out to all.

ABOUT THE AUTHOR

MARK O'CONNELL RECENTLY retired from Virginia's Department of Community Corrections after serving 25 years as a Probation/Parole Officer. He is married and the father of three adult children. He works as a freelance sports reporter to a couple of newspapers and as a sports commentator for a local television station. He is also involved in a youth mentoring program. This is his second book. His first, *Criminal Minds in Real Time*, was recently published.

Contact him via email at takedownnews@aol.com

listen|imagine|view|experience

CPSIA information can be obtained
at www.ICGtesting.com
Printed in the USA
FSOW02n1025140916
25002FS

NOV - - 2016

9 781683 523413